DEVIL ON THE LOOSE

By

Doug Hocking

Buckland Abbey, L.L.C.

Devil on the Loose

www.doughocking.com

Published by
Buckland Abbey, L.L.C.
Sierra Vista, Arizona
Cover Layout and Design

Cover Photo Credit
Wyatt's Hotel, Coffee House and Saloon Theatre

This is a work of fiction. Some of the characters, organizations, and events portrayed in this novel are taken from actual history; and some within are products of the author's imagination or are used fictitiously.

ISBN: 978-0-9907619-4-5
LCCN: 2016901028

Other Books by Doug Hocking

***Massacre at Point of Rocks*, 2013.** The story of Kit Carson and the White wagon train massacre. Ann White and her baby daughter were taken captive by Jicarilla Apache in 1849. The Army recruited a reluctant Kit Carson to get her back. The trail was three weeks old and it had snowed, but Kit followed it for over 200 miles. The story takes the reader into Jicarilla Apache camps and ceremonies and explores what life was like in 1949. Available from www.doughocking.com , Amazon.com and Ingram.

***The Mystery of Chaco Canyon*, 2014.** Four friends, an Anglo, two New Mexicans and a Jicarilla Apache are set on a quest after a fabulous treasure. The trail will lead them all over the Southwest of the early 1860s, and through Civil War battles as they are pursued by Penitentes, Danites and Knights of the Golden Circle all seeking the same long lost power. The story starts at a rock in Los Lunas, New Mexico, where the Ten Commandments are inscribed in an ancient Hebrew dialect. Available from www.doughocking.com , Amazon.com and Ingram.

***The Wildest West*, 2016.** A collection of short material set in the Wild Southwest of the 1850s and 60s when there was no law and the west was wild. Revolvers were new and men fought with tomahawks and muzzle loading weapons. Available from www.doughocking.com , Amazon.com and Ingram.

***Tom Jeffords, Friend of Cochise*, 2017.** Jimmy Stewart played Tom Jeffords in 1950's *Broken Arrow* to Jeff Chandler's Cochise. He rode alone into Cochise's Stronghold to make the peace. The real Jeffords was equally brave and became fast friends with the chief. The history books got most of it wrong. The true story is even better.

Dedication

To my wife, **Debbie Erno Hocking**, who puts up with it all and tries to help

And to my editor, **Adele Brinkley**, who translates my Cornish into English

And to my children, **Eric and Jenne**, and six grandkids: **Mecia, Asia, Tichina, Dearron, Olivia and Eva**

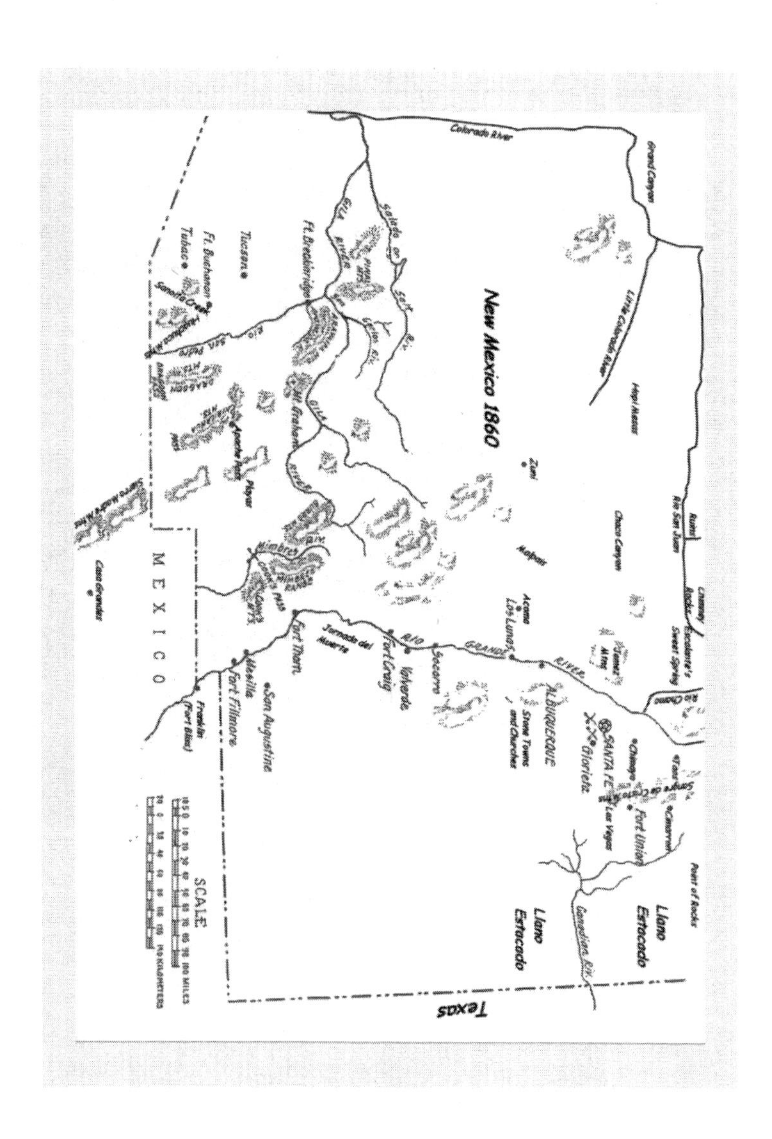
New Mexico 1860
Colorado River
Grand Canyon
Little Colorado River
Hopi Mesas
Zuni
Chaco Canyon
Acoma
Los Lunas
RIO GRANDE RIVER
ALBUQUERQUE
SANTA FE
Glorieta
Fort Union
Point of Rocks
Llano Estacado
Llano Estacado
Texas
MEXICO
Jornada del Muerto
Socorro
Valverde
Fort Craig
Fort Thorn
Mesilla
Fort Fillmore
San Augustine
Franklin (Fort Bliss)
Tucson
Ft. Buchanan
Tubac
Ft. Breckinridge
Casa Grandes
SCALE

Arizona in 1860

Chapter 1 - On the Dodge

The cool, high altitude, night air brought thoughts to a man's mind. Crispy and mostly clear with a hint of piñon and chili, it made a man think about the future. He couldn't just exist from day to day. He ought to make something of himself. Planning for the short term was my strong suit. Planning for the future was a distant wish that only came when desert stars shone bright. Home, wife, family, and wealth seemed far off as remote as the stars, but one never knows what life will bring. I moved toward the dim light ahead.

Smoke hung thick in the Exchange Hotel's *sala.* That's the one on the Plaza at the end of the Santa Fe Trail, the one the Mexicans call *La Fonda*, the inn. I stood to the bar, *elbow crookin'* and puffing on my nose-warmer. Piñon from the *horno* in the corner and cigar blended to burn the eyes, assault the sinuses, and please the palate. Piñon hinted of cooking beans and roasted meat. The pleasant aroma of roasting chilis and tortillas could hardly compete. Light was poor in the adobe room; only a few lanterns pushed back the gloom. Overhead vigas blackened with age and smoke reflected only smudge. In the recesses, musicians were beating a sad Mexican love song near to death to the accompaniment of excited shouting from the gamblers at the monte tables. One voice cut through it all like a foghorn.

"Aubry was a liar and a scoundrel who never did half the things he claimed!"

The speaker was a big man with darting gray eyes that lacked signs of clear resolution. He was a man who would choose the easy path. His body showed it, too.

Although powerful looking, there was flab pressing over his belt and rounding the seat of his pants. He dressed well in city clothes: black frock coat, ruffled shirt, and red silk vest. He didn't show signs of having done much hard work anytime recently. How Bane Helligan made his living was unclear. He would have said land speculation. He'd speculate that the crop was in and then run some poor Mexican off the land. A gang of toughs had gathered round him, together disappearing from town for days only to return with fresh money to spend. Rumors abounded. People feared the "Association."

Not long before a friend had asked me to look into the whereabouts of his missing livestock. I followed what seemed a promising trail and rode up a canyon finding myself unexpectedly in Helligan's camp. He wasn't happy to see me. No beeves were in sight and I couldn't go further since he blocked the trail. Although certain he had stolen the animals, I had to turn back.

"Francis Xavier Aubry was my friend," I heard myself say with clear belligerence. "And it's *kicklish* for a *boggler* to shame him in my presence unless he wants a *basting*. The Skimmer of the Prairies rode from here to Independence in five and half days!" That was the claim most usually disputed. "And he did much more besides." I was ashamed that Helligan and many of his men carried West Country, Cornish, names. From the sound of their talk, none of them were recent arrivals. Thank the saints for small favors. I didn't wish to be connected with them, and there were few enough Cousin Jacks in this land.

The original comment might have been made to the world at large, or Bane might have been trying to prod me, thinking I knew too much. It didn't matter. Folks knew how I felt about FX Aubry. Things stood to get *oogly*.

"You disputin' me, runt?" came the counter charge.

I'm a big man, broad in the shoulder and powerful, over six feet, but next to Bane I seemed much smaller. He had a roomful of associates, and I was alone.

"Tha's right," I replied. "And I'll thank the likes of you not to tarnish his memory by mouthing his name. I never knew a better man than Captain Aubry so *truss up yer clapper, wifflehead*, unless yer planning to leave here in a wheel *barra*."

FX Aubry died in August of 1854, at Mercure's store just a few doors away. It'd been a situation not unlike this one. Weightman had been a little drunk, while the captain, who had just arrived, was on his first drink. They talked in a friendly way until FX asked Weightman what had happened to that newspaper he used to edit.

"It went out of business," Weightman replied.

"Good," said Captain Aubry. "A lying rag like that should go out of business."

Weightman had disparaged some of Aubry's accomplishments. Now it was Weightman's turn to be angry.

"Take that back!" he roared, towering over Aubry who, though handsome and impeccably dressed, was only five foot three and barely 100 pounds.

Challenged, Aubry went for his Colt. It misfired, they said. But I've never seen a misfire go into the ceiling. I think it was a warning shot. Knowing FX, I think, he was hoping Weightman would soil himself. Instead, Weightman drew his knife and closed the distance. Aubry had time for a second shot, but he didn't take it. Weightman drove his knife in and twisted it, real deliberate like, until the captain was dead. The authorities ruled his murder self-defense.

The muscles of Bane's face bunched in rage, and his ugly visage turned red. "No man talks to me like that," he growled as the room went silent, "and lives."

When men have been drinking, as Bane had, tempers flare. I figured there'd be a *capperause*, a dust up; *howsumever,* Bane drew his revolver, and I heard it click to full cock as I drew my Bowie. I heard the hammer fall as well. Missing percussion cap? Empty cylinder? I didn't have time to investigate as the hammer clicked back to full-cock a second time. I, like Weightman before me, closed the distance, knocking his muzzle aside, and gutted the brute. His lights poured out in a lump, staining his red vest a darker shade. The air stank of the privy. The knife pierced his bowel. The pistol spoke searing my side, igniting my shirt, adding the acrid stench of sulfur and dense smoke to the gloom. Swinging my heavy knife around, I brought it down hard, blade first, on the wrist of his gun hand. I'm not clear as to whether he managed two screams or only one long bellow. The knife cut deep, and he dropped the gun. It would take him a while to die, and that belly cut would hurt like hell. He fell to the floor with a wet plop and landed in his own blood. I turned and walked out into the night, beating out my smoldering shirt. It stung.

As I went, I heard O'Malley, one of the associates - a man like Bane Helligan doesn't have friends - saying, "He disarmed Bane. Then he cut open his stomach."

Another, cried out, "Disarmed? Bane didn't have a gun." I suppose an associate had taken it. It was beginning to sound as if I wouldn't be as fortunate as Weightman. It seemed O'Malley was next to in line to head the gang. He lacked Helligan's style and cleverness, though he was just as mean and would want to avenge the leader to cement his position.

He was big, though not so big as Helligan, and muscular. He wore his filthy, red-checked shirt with a cowhide vest and Mexican sombrero. He wore one Colt's revolver strapped down low and carried a Bowie. He concealed another smaller gun in his clothes. I'd seen it once, a pepperbox. Like all thieves he was basically lazy, but he wasn't so successful at being lazy as his boss was.

It seemed to me now might be a good time to leave Santa Fe. I'd heard of a place called Tubac down in the Gadsden Purchase. Though still part of New Mexico Territory, in December 1858, Tubac was as remote from Santa Fe as any South Sea Island, and folks were mining silver and gold at Cerro Gordo and in the Santa Rita Mountains. Where there was ore, there was opportunity. By all accounts, the law didn't reach any farther than Mesilla, 300 miles short of Tubac. Desperate characters from New Mexico and California headed into the Purchase to avoid arrest.

I woke the liveryman and asked him to saddle my strawberry roan. He sold me a pack mule and accepted a healthy tip with a smile. I gathered my bedroll and a few things, two Colt Dragoon revolvers, a Walker Colt, a Hawken rifle, and some clothing, including a fleece lined leather coat and a capote, an overcoat made of Hudson Bay blankets that I wore in the worst weather. The Hawken was a state-of-the-art muzzle-loading, percussion-cap rifle. The Colts were also percussion cap. They'd take a deuced long time to reload, but I'd have 18 shots before I found the need.

I beat on the *zaguan*, the big, red gate that admitted wagons to the inner courtyard, at the Spiegelberg Store.

From the window above, I heard younger-brother Levi's German accented voice, "Go avay. Ve ist closdt! Can't you zee?"

"Levi, it's me!" I called up. "I'm callin' in a favor."

"Ja! Ist ze. I lets you in," he replied.

Half an hour later, my mule was packed with a few tools, salt, flour, sugar, coffee, ammunition, tins of food, and a few things I thought might sell at a profit down the line. The brothers hugged me and wished me well when I explained why I had to leave in the middle of a snowy December night.

"Scout ze place for us," said Moshe. "Maybe we makes a store zere zoon."

Behind me, I could hear shouts as the Association scoured the town looking for me. Lanterns and torches gave away their positions, and they were easy to avoid. I was ready and splashed across the Agua Fria. As I rode south, I thought about what I'd do in the Purchase. When I drove stock out to California with Captain Aubry in 1852, I learned a lot about gold mining. It's a rare prospector indeed who gets rich off his finds. Placer mines require a lot of water and backbreaking work. Only the best placers pay off well. A miner had to develop load prospects in hard rock before they were worth anything, and development took big money. That's where the speculators got rich.

A mine owner is a man from a class of liars in ownership of a hole in the ground; they promote their "mines" to investors mostly back east. They rise and fall spectacularly winning and losing fortunes. Those who labor over a sluice box with a shovel have the thrill of picking gold up free off the ground in exchange for a great deal of hard work. Those who really get rich off a gold rush are those who provide food, like the stock we took to California, and supplies, the merchants, freighters, gamblers, and whores, who provide entertainment. There are a lot of ways to get rich in a gold rush; mining those poor souls who toil underground wasn't one of them. I lacked talent with cards and the build for whoring, so handling stock, or merchandise it would have to be. I'd learned a lot about both stock and trade while riding with Aubry. Something would turn up; it always did.

Santa Fe and the Rio Arriba were no longer safe.

They'd be looking for a man who spoke in Cornish tones, so I'd have to conceal my accent, at least for a while. There weren't many of us, and my speech would be a distinguishing feature. Fortunately, I promised myself, they wouldn't search either long or far. Saint Peran, patron of Cornwall and tin miners, he who'd walked across the Irish Sea with a millstone chained to his leg, wasn't looking over me on this one. The situation was about to be overcome by events. Perhaps it's because I'm a West Country Dissenter, a Methodist, whom the Catholic saint wants no part of, though you'd think a saint as fond o' bitter as Peran would bless any West Country boy.

Ah well, I thought, what did it all matter to a man who rode alone without a care? I lit me nose-warmer and puffed contentedly.

Swirling *bacca* smoke brought with it dreams of home far away. I'd oft sucked me nose-warmer in a favored public house on the Cornish coast among friends, crew, and fellow captains cheering our success as smugglers and clever men. Family was there, too, but then I preferred a swift boat and a sharp crew laughing as we left the Royal Navy in our wake. But there's only so much 'is Majesty's jollies will take. Fame does not mean fortune, but it is dangerous. Rising makes a captain visible and a target. Not caring to have my neck made any longer than it is now, I departed my snug harbor a much wanted man.

Trail dust, old leather, and horse sweat filled my nostrils reminding me of other times spent chasing the guidon of Company G, 1st Dragoons, behind Captain Richard Ewell. There was no finer captain anywhere, and those months under him were shining times as I learned to fight Indians and outlaws and stay alive.

I looked up at the dark skies and bright stars. Where would they lead me? Would there be home, wealth, friends, and, most important, love where I was bound? My roan snorted. Was that sound he made disgust?

Chapter 2 - Jornada del Muerte

I rode south through the night. The descent over the escarpment from Santa Fe at 7,000 feet down to Santo Domingo in the *Abajo* at 4,800 took me from winter back to early fall. It was a good change that made traveling a pleasure. The *Rio Abajo* was not only south of Santa Fe but thousands of feet lower. Elevation made a difference in this country. Riding through the *Abajo*, I followed the Great River of the North, the Rio Grande del Norte, passing Bernalillo and Albuquerque. The land was green with farms near the river and meadows for grazing further back, a good land of small villages and large *haciendas*. The men of the *Rio Arriba*, the north, were free but perhaps a little mad. They had fomented two revolutions in recent years. In the south, the *Abajo*, life was more peaceful, though the people were either *ricos*, the wealthy, or their tenants and *peones*, working off debts in servitude. The *Abajo* was a green ribbon through a desert land.

Fondas, inns, were rare. In Mexican times, the caravans ran only once per year, in Spanish times perhaps one year in three. The Mexicans were not so fiddle-footed as *gavachos*, as they called Americans, and times were lean for landlords. The new Santa Fe-Mesilla Mail Coach carried passengers and mail to the Butterfield Overland Mail connection at Mesilla twice per week. That run was a remnant of the San Antonio-San Diego Jackass mail that had preceded the Butterfield. Some of the stations offered food, but I wasn't sure which ones. Continuing an ancient tradition, the *hacendados* of the big *ranchos* took in travelers and in this way got the latest news and gossip. I worked my way slowly south, letting my stock graze and fatten. There would be hard times after Fort Craig as we crossed the 100-mile *Jornada del Muerte*, the Journey of the Dead.

By all accounts, the Jornada was devoid of water and grass and full of Mescalero Apaches. The Rio Grande dipped into a canyon, and the ground was mostly impassable. Several deep, nearly impassable, canyons came in from the west. Wagons and *carretas* left the river and followed the Jornada. Since earliest times, *El Camino Real*, the Royal Road, had detoured east of the mountains deep into Apacheland on a road that was easy for wagons but devoid of water. The alternative was a mountainous detour west along Cooke's Road, avoiding the Mescalero but coming to grips with the Mimbres, Gila, Red Forehead, or Warm Springs People. Whichever name you choose to call them, they were still Apaches. Their leaders were *Cuchillo Negro*, Black Knife, and the giant, *Mangas Coloradas*, Red Sleeves. There is no need to speculate on what made his sleeves red. Lone travelers seldom arrived at their expected destinations. A canny voyager waited for a group of 20 or 30 to form.

The Apache liked fights that they were sure to win with few losses. Perhaps that was why they didn't attack the Overland Mail. There is no great trick to stopping a stagecoach: shoot one of the horses of the lead team, block the road at a narrow defile, or simply catch it crawling up a steep grade. Highwaymen had been using these tactics for years, maybe centuries. The Apache didn't want gold or pocket watches, so there was little of value to them on a coach. Furthermore, seven to nine heavily-armed travelers rode in a stagecoach. For the Apache, stopping the

Butterfield was like knocking down a hornet's nest: not much sense to it and a good chance of getting stung.

I didn't think O'Malley and his friends had the energy or the inclination to follow me. I couldn't be sure, but the possibility didn't seem likely. O'Malley, I thought, was busy consolidating his criminal enterprises and picking up the threads of whatever ties Bane Helligan had with fences and officialdom. There was little need for speed, I thought, riding south, only a need to find a new place to live and a new way to make a living. Staying in Santa Fe would have been an affront to the gang, and O'Malley would see to it that I was slain. But, out of sight, out of mind, and I was safe away from their haunts. Or so I thought.

My horse plodded south through the lush river valley, happy to be growing fat on rich winter grass and easy riding. A horse starts a trek with lots of muscle, fat, and meat along his backbone. On long journeys, the fat and then the muscle are lost. Every day, the saddle settles down a little further until its hard parts are rubbing against his back, galling it. The horse develops saddle sores and soon isn't much good. Captain McClellan had developed a saddle that had a gap down the middle so it wouldn't rub the horse. It wasn't very comfortable, but as he said, "If you wanted comfort, you shouldn't have joined the dragoons." We plodded on toward Socorro, which meant "relief." It was the first town after the dry Jornada.

At Fort Craig, I picked up a bit of luck and some unsettling news.

The bad news came first: two of Helligan's brothers, Jacko and Tallon, who had arrived from Texas to join Bane in "business." They'd passed through Fort Craig on their way a week before I got there. Luck kept us from meeting on the trail, although they wouldn't have known me. Now my slow progress south allowed the news from Santa Fe to get ahead of me. Reliable reports said that the Helligans were extremely disappointed at finding Bane dead, and Jacko had supplanted O'Malley as head of the gang. The reports described him as being six foot four, broad shouldered, hawked-nosed, jet-haired, and mean, and they said he was smarter than his younger brother was. Maybe, but 6'4" was probably stretching things, I hoped. Tallon was even bigger and heavily muscled, though not as smart as his brothers were. Worse, they'd brought along two cousins, Hellyar and Turk Pellewe. They were Arkansas feuding men by all accounts, even if they carried West Country names. Unlike O'Malley, the quartet wanted me dead. They'd put out word and were offering money and favors for news of my whereabouts.

Approaching me was a young man in a neat, clean, and pressed officer's uniform with pistol and saber at his side. "Sir," Lieutenant Averell said, "I've been assigned to escort the stage through the *Jornada del Muerte*. I hear you're headed that way. You're more than welcome to come along."

Lieutenant William Averell was only a year out of West Point.

One of the dragoon sergeants had recognized me. "That lieutenant's all right. He'd only been in New Mexico a few days when Mescaleros attacked a ranch three miles south of here. The lieutenant took out a detachment and actually managed to make contact with them. He's earned quite a reputation as an Indian fighter."

Sadly, most missions sent out after the fact saw no Indians and at best returned with a little worn out stock. The Lieutenant actually succeeded in killing a few Apache raiders.

Averell asked again, and I responded, “I’d like that, Lieutenant.”

“I got to warn you, sir,” Averell said, “most of my troops are green. This will be their first mission. I really can use a good, steady fighter like you.”

I looked at him quizzically. I was laying low, not giving out my name. I wondered if he’d recognized me, but his next question reassured me he’d only made a visual assessment of my clothing and gear. I was worried. The news that the Helligans were seeking me came hard. I’d have to be careful about making my presence known, at least until I got beyond Mesilla. Then I’d be safe. The sergeant hadn’t said anything about who I was. That was good.

“What is your name, sir?” the lieutenant asked.

“*Sin nombre*,” I mumbled. I had to think fast. It was the first thing that came to my mind, though I hated lying to him. *Sin nombre* is Mexican for without a name. I was mumbling my thoughts out loud about concealing myself, and Sin Nombre became my new name. It took me a few moments to work out the spelling, St. Gnomebray, sort of Anglo-French like St. Claire which is pronounced Sinclair.

“St. Gnomebray,” I said.

“Sinombre?” he queried.

“No, s-t for Saint,” I explained. “Like St. John which is pronounced “sin gin,” or St. Claire, which is pronounced Sinclair. And Gnomebray, g-n-o-m-e-b-r-a-y, but the g is silent. He was a Celtic saint, but no one remembers his name, except my family. The church didn't like him carrying on with the "little people," the gnomes and the *piskies*."

Uh oh, I'd have to be careful about calling the little people *piskies*. Only a Cornishman would do that and there weren't many of us around. Everyone else calls them pixies. Only in Cornwall do we call them *piskies*. Someone might recall the peculiarities of my speech. An accent is easy to ape. After years in New Mexico, I fell easily into the local cant, a mix of Mexican words and Southern drawl. But the expressions of one's youth stay with a man unbidden, hidden, and mixed with the common tongue. For now, the deal was done. I'd have an escort as far as Mesilla.

The journey was uneventful though unpleasant, although the lieutenant proved a worthy companion. The stage line had dug wells and tanks, so we had water, and the company had put in change stations. We stopped nights to rest the lieutenant's horses and dragoons. They were an odd, noisy lot. Germans, Irish, men who'd failed in love or business and adventurers off to see the world. On the whole, they seemed good hearted and brave though unready for New Mexico. Their gear, sabers, single shot horse pistols, musketoons, and canteens clattered and banged scaring off game and Indians. The musketoon was a sort of sawed off musket. Having no rifling, it had little more range and accuracy than a pistol. Their polished metal gleamed in the sunlight and shot flashes that could be seen forty miles away. They wore blue uniforms with shiny buttons and yellow facings. The facings should have been orange showing they were dragoons and stood far above the common lot, but the new uniform was still rare as hen's teeth out west.

Always alert for things that moved in the night, we sat away from the fire. I sat with my back to it, as did their sergeants, keeping my night vision by not looking into the fire. Some of the new men seemed to think my behavior standoffish, but it was lifesaving in Apache country.

"Have you got a bit of *bacca* for me nose-warmer?" I asked.

A dragoon looked at me quizzically and I clarified. "Tobacco for my pipe." He did, but I'd have to mind the Cornish rhythms of my speech.

One of the dragoons tried to explain the nature of their regiment to me. "You see, sir," he said, "first comes the President, then comes the general, then comes the general's horse. After the general's horse come the dragoons. After the dragoons comes nothing, and after nothing comes the infantry. It was a company of dragoons defeated Santy Anna's whole 20,000-man army at Buena Vista. I heard General Taylor said so hisself."

"Buena Vista was a glorious victory," I said. I closed my eyes and recalled the scenes of volunteers running, then standing, and going back into the line to face the Mexicans again. Great Western challenged those who ran to stand and fight. She carried many from the field herself to give them care. Sarah Bowman, flame-haired and over six feet tall, was quite a woman. They called her Great Western after the largest and most beautiful ship of the day. The "flying" artillery was everywhere, filling gaps in the line like an infantry reserve and terrifying the Mexicans. The 1st Dragoons, too, were everywhere from one end of the field to the other. I'd been a boy like this dragoon in

'46. The San Patricios were there, too, Irish-Catholic deserters fighting for the Mexicans against their former comrades. Give the Devil his due; it was the first time we saw Mexican artillery served with anything like efficiency.

I was only a boy, like this one, direct from the boat. Unable to find work, I'd enlisted in the 1st Dragoons and fought through a war. Afterward, the Dragoons had brought me to newly acquired New Mexico where I learned to fight Indians, mostly Navajos and Jicarilla Apache. I'd stayed on, putting Cornish mining skills to work and learning about livestock.

"Dragoons is the elite!" the boy pronounced waking me from my reverie.

I returned my gaze to the dark night sky and brilliant stars, smiling at his enthusiasm. *Bacca* smoke drifted heavenward mixing with thin clouds. I tugged my capote tight around me and wondered what tomorrow would bring. I'd like to find a lass. I was getting a bit long in the tooth to marry, not that 35 is really that old. What would a girl want with me, especially the kind of fine, pretty girl I would want? I had few prospects and no land, money, or job. Maybe I'd find something in Tubac.

Chapter 3 - Mesilla

Mesilla was the biggest town south of Albuquerque. I heard Mexicans who came south so they could stay in Mexico had founded it after the Mexican War. It didn't work out for them, and they were somewhat surprised when the army established Fort Fillmore a few miles north of their new town in '52 and when the dragoons raised the flag in the plaza taking possession of the Gadsden Purchase. The town was the county seat of Doña Ana County, which stretched from New Mexico's eastern border with Texas, wherever that uncertain line was (Texas said at the Rio Grande), west to the Colorado River. It included all of the Gadsden Purchase and then some. For folks in Tucson and Tubac, it meant that criminal cases had to be brought 300 miles to Mesilla once or twice a year when the court "visited" from Santa Fe. That made Tucson a haven for people who wanted no part of the law. There were no towns between Mesilla and Tucson.

Mesilla was a dusty, Mexican town on the west bank of the Rio Grande, a plaza of boxy, adobe buildings with flat rooves and no windows. Glass was at a premium. Those who brought it over the Santa Fe Trail passed on the great expense to their customers. There were a few American merchants, but even they didn't have shop windows you could browse. Unlike the Mexican competition, they did hang out signs. One of the largest buildings, besides the church, was the Overland Mail Building. Four stages ran through every week, two in each direction.

I found a blacksmith shop run by a man from Pennsylvania and had him check my horse's and mule's shoes and tack. It would be better to replace a shoe now than to have it thrown on the trail. It would be a long ride to Tubac. While I was there, word of a stranger in town spread or at least spread along the lines of someone's web. He came to welcome me. I found his approach overly forward, but perhaps that was just my English upbringing. Westerners are more headfirst and in more of a hurry.

"Palatine, I'm called," said the stranger approaching me. Of medium height the man was average, brown hair, brown eyes, and medium build. He leaned toward pretty, caring for his slick hair and nails more than most men would. His dark suit was clean and cut with a bit of flamboyance, and his tooled Mexican boots polished. A gambler or saloon keeper, I thought, maybe a flash merchant or mine stock swindler. Instead of meeting my gaze, his eyes darted to and fro, taking in whoever might be observing us. Gambling and saloon keeping were honest enough professions, even respected in the Southwest, but I did not trust this man. A girl followed him dressed like an Apache but far too light skinned. Thin and frightened, she looked about 14-years-old.

"Palatine Robinson," he went on, "from Tucson. I'm told you're headed there." His voice had a slight southern twang, Kentucky perhaps. "I'm getting up a poker game for tonight right over there at the *sala*," he said, pointing, and then extending his hand toward me.

Ordinarily, I would have avoided the game and the attention it might bring, but the play was a chance to learn more about the country to which I was bound.

"I appreciate the invitation," I replied politely without committing myself. "But you've been misinformed. I'm bound east for San Antonio." I could see no point in leaving obvious tracks that anyone could follow. After all, Helligan's kin had arrived in Santa Fe by all accounts. They must have been on the way long before my confrontation with Bane. Perhaps Bane thought he had some big score lined up. The only force in New Mexico that could oppose him was the Army. The local sheriffs and courts left much to be desired. They operated under Federal law, which protected the rights of outlaws over citizens.

The plaza was small but offered a variety of cantinas, the food Mexican of fair quality, and several stores, the largest displaying a sign reading "A.J. Fountain." The chilis here could not compare to Chimayo's, and the preparation in the cantinas could not equal that of Santa Fe, but it was better than rough food often eaten cold along the trail. I found the Butterfield Station on the west side outside the plaza south of Fountain's store and talked to the station keepers, Emmett Mills and Freeman Thomas, about the schedule.

"Call me Free," said the man in tones that told me he was from New York. Many Butterfield men were. "Of course, you can ride along with the stage. It's Apache country. Glad of an extra gun, although we've never really had any trouble."

I smiled. "What does 'really' mean?"

"Well, there have been some personal scuffles and knife fights. Tevis helped a Mexican captive, Merijildo Grijalva, escape on board a stage. That really upset Cochise. His people have promised to kill everyone at the Apache Pass Station a couple of times."

"Yeah," said Emmett Mills, a boy still in his teens, "and when we first opened up Stein's Peak Station, Mangas Coloradas showed up with all his men and wouldn't leave until we gave him all the cornmeal we had and some other things, too. Damn thieves." He spat unconvincingly into the dust. He was a young man trying to seem tough and older.

"We don't really get many passengers," Free went on. "The station keepers along the way will be glad to have your company and an extra hand with some of the work. You can rest your horses at the stations. You'll never be able to follow one stage all the way. They only stop to change horses and eat. Nine miles an hour they run!"

My journey would take longer, but I still thought I had the time. The Helligans wouldn't trace me beyond Mesilla.

At *kindle teening*, I set out looking for a bite to eat. I'd have to watch that. "Candle trimming time" is what we Cornish call the dusk. If I spoke it aloud, someone was apt to notice. *Kindle teening* was time to cure the *collywobbles,* so I sought a *fulsome* dinner at the cleanest looking of the eateries, La Posta. Mexicans served *Posole* in a bowl with tortillas, which they used as spoons. *Carne asada* came rolled in tortillas set directly on the table. Flatware was unheard of in these parts, likewise plates. I stuffed myself. Good food would be rare where I was headed.

In full dark, I made my way to the *sala,* the gambling hall, nearby. A serape was hung in lieu of door. The windowless, dirt floored, adobe room was dim inside. The only light provided by a few candles hung in tinware holders; tin cans brought across the Santa Fe Trail were turned into useful art. A *banco* lined three sides of the room providing seating; the "bar," planks supported by barrels, took up the fourth wall. The packed earth floor showed stains from tobacco chewers, and the ceiling's *vigas* and *latillas* were coated in soot. The room, only 12 feet wide, the most the *vigas* could support, ran deep and smoke from *cigaritos* and pipes filled the air. In luxury, three aged tables with chairs dominated the center of the room. Palatine Robinson sat at one beckoning me, his girl standing behind him.

I ordered whiskey at the bar and made my way to the table, wondering about the drink. Beer was a rarity. It's brewing was a skill and required ice as part of the process. Mexicans didn't know how to brew it. They made *pulque* and *mescal* from the century plant. The stuff tasted awful. Whiskey came in barrels, and to save weight and bulk on the trail, it was sent out close to pure. The saloonkeeper would add water, brown sugar, and tobacco to give it color and flavor. Sometimes they felt compelled to add other things for flavor, such as rattlesnake heads, scorpions, cactus, and Sacred Datura flowers. Such recipes could be dangerous and produce strange side effects. In any event, the whiskey was green, not aged a bit, which meant it went down hard and produced a splitting head, guaranteed. Sure they served it in bottles to make you think it was the good stuff, but they filled them from the big barrel out back.

At Palatine's table, the game was *pokar* played with a Spanish deck: 40 cards, the pips were 1 to 7 with no 8, 9, or 10, the suits were coins, swords, clubs, and cups, and the royals were Jack, Horse, and King. The game may have been Spanish, but the players were not, though I've forgotten the names of the Texians who joined us. The deck was dog eared and greasy. A new deck was a luxury, so I watched for peculiarities in Palatine's deck.

After losing a few pots, I spotted his simple marking system and slowly began to press him, winning only a little at first. The Texians didn't pick up on it and lost heavily. Two seemed to know each other well. The third was younger and a stranger.

A Mexican in a dirty outfit sat on the *banco* watching our table. He wore tooled leather pantaloons closed at the side with silver concho buttons, a shirt that might once have been white, and a black velvet vest with silver buttons. A broad-brimmed sombrero cast his face in shadow. A large knife stuck in a red sash and a Colt revolver completed his outfit. Robinson didn't acknowledge him, but I thought they were allies from the way the vaquero watched our table.

As we played, Palatine Robinson talked, as I'd hoped.

"Most of the population is down by an old *presidio* at Tubac, tending the mines in the Santa Rita Mountains and at Cerro Colorado," he said. "The rest lives in Tucson or spread out along the Rio Santa Cruz and Sonoita Creek where they farm and raise cattle to support the mines. Fort Buchanan is at the head of Sonoita Creek, and Sylvester Mowry has got a mine at Patagonia nearby. Apart from that, it's all Apaches. There's nothing for 300 miles except for Butterfield Stations until you get to Mesilla. That Sylvester, what a guy. He used to be army."

I wondered if he was prodding at my background.

"Sylvester Mowry had to be rescued from Utah by the army," Palatine said. I knew the story. He'd seduced the daughter-in-law of Brigham Young while her husband was away on mission. "He showed me his book once. He keeps notes comparing the qualities of different Indian tribes by how good their women are in bed."

I knocked back my whiskey in one shot. It was *oogly*. No telling what was in it. I stepped to the bar and ordered mescal, cactus liquor, and nursed it slowly but with a flourish giving the impression that I was drinking much more than I was. The others drank more heavily than a good *pokar* player should and soon were a bit *taddly-oodly*.

His lips loosened by liquor, Palatine talked on. "It's wild country. There is no law. It's every man for hisself. The closest law or government comes is here in Mesilla. The country is wide open. Even Mexican bandits come north raiding, not to mention Apaches. In October, Mexican employees building the Butterfield Station at Dragoon Springs killed the American workers and almost cut off Silas St. John's arm. He kept them at bay, and it was nine days before he got medical attention from Fort Buchanan. They took his arm, but in days he was working again. That's the kind of man it takes to survive in Arizona."

"Sounds like the devil's on the loose," I said. "It's *Tantarabobus's* own playground and a place to avoid." Blast all, I'd used the Cornish name for the devil.

Palatine steadied his eyes and looked hard at me. "A man with cunning and courage can make his fortune."

The Texians were growing angry. They began to grumble and curse but continued drinking. I pressed harder in the game. Pressing hard was not so difficult when you knew the cards the other player was holding, even though he knew yours. Palatine's stake began to dwindle but so did that of the Texas boys. I could see Palatine growing suspicious, no poker face behind the liquor, but he hardly dared say anything since the marked deck was his own.

One Texian who could barely steady his eyes pointed at Palatine and then me. "You're cheating, you bastards! You're in it together!"

I could hardly deny cheating, even if in self-defense. Palatine roared, “Sir! No man calls me a bastard and lives!”

The Texian jumped to his feet and reached for his weapon. The Mexican’s pistol roared and the Texian fell to the floor. His drunken compatriots looked surprised. They weren’t ready for gunplay.

Palatine now held a pepperbox and had it pointed at the Texians. “Take your friend out of here.” They dragged him out the door, were gone for a few minutes, and then returned to continue play. I guess he wasn’t their friend after all. Dumping a friend’s body and continuing to play cards seemed a bit much. In Santa Fe, the *fandango* was over when the first man got stabbed. In the Purchase, it didn’t seem to make a difference. Truly, the devil was on the loose in this land they were starting to call Arizona.

There was no law in Mesilla, and no one to conduct an inquest. The shooting went unchallenged but probably would have been called a fair fight, even though the Mexican’s stepping-in came as a surprise.

I now knew that Palatine Robinson cheated at cards and guns. He’d always have protection. Unbelievably, he suggested continuing the game. I could hardly refuse. He was down, and I was up. I could hardly deny him a chance to win back what he’d lost.

The game went on. Knowing both of us held good hands, though his was the better of the two, I took a risk and raised him more than he had showing on the table.

“Please accept my marker,” he said.

“I’m sorry, I can’t,” I replied politely. “I won’t be in town that long.”

"Then, here," said Palatine, "take this girl. Surely she's worth the amount. She's a Pima held captive by the Apache and sold to me by that warrior race."

"Now hold on," I replied. "She looks Mexican to me. Besides, slavery is illegal in New Mexico. Against the law."

"Ah, but not enforced," he smiled. "Many men bring their black slaves, and the Mexicans trade in Indian slaves at all times. Always have."

The Mexicans didn't call it slavery. They claimed to be taking in the poor, benighted *cimarrones*, wild Indians, to teach them Christianity and civilization. Holding a Mexican in slavery was a horse of a different color. The *hacendados* did accept *peones*, debt slaves, but that wasn't quite the same.

"I expect to cross some rough country," I said. "I can't take her with me."

That ended the game. I swept in the pot as he couldn't call the hand. He held better cards, but they remained face down. The Texians didn't look happy about any of it.

The next day I crossed the Rio Grande and rode south along the Overland Trail as far as Fort Fillmore before making a wide loop west, crossing the river again. I then headed back north. Stopping to rest, I saw dust of men riding hard toward the south on the Overland Trail where I'd just come from. They were across the river from my position. Concealing my livestock, and myself I watched as a mile distant Palatine, a big Mexican, and two Texians from last night's game rode by, making hard for Fort Fillmore. Either Palatine had convinced them I was the one cheating, or they'd been in it with him.

When they had passed, I waved my hat and wished them *bon chance* and threw in a wish that they might be *piskie-led* in the wilds.

Chapter 4 - The Road to Dragoon Springs

I began the long ride to the silver mining country around Tubac 300 miles away, skirting Mesilla on my way north and stopping at Picacho Station. The Butterfield Stations were a string of pearls stretching across the New Mexico desert every fifteen to twenty-five miles all the way from Fort Fillmore to Fort Yuma on the California side of the Colorado River.

Colorado means the red river of the west. The Mexicans only have a very few names for rivers: Colorado, red, Blanco, white, Negro, black, Verde, green, Salado, salty, Cimarron, wild, Cañada, in a canyon, Grande, big, Animas, spooky meaning someone drowned there, and Puerco, filthy. There are three filthy (Rio Puerco) rivers between Zuñi, Albuquerque, and Abiquiu alone. It's no wonder travelers get confused. They also change the name of the river depending on where they come upon it. In Texas, the Rio Grande del Norte is the Rio Bravo, no longer grand, merely brave, and the Rio Cañada of New Mexico becomes the Red (Colorado of the Llano) in Texas, presumably because out on prairies, it ran out of canyons to limp through.

Picacho, the butte, stood like a sentinel in the desert, visible for many miles, a requirement, along with reliable water and good grass, for Butterfield stations.

A voice distinctly canted toward New England and New York cried out from the door of the windowless adobe station, "Rider coming!" Two others looked up from feeding and watering mules to see if what approached brought menace then went about their business.

These were brave men. Two or three would live alone in Apache country far beyond the reach of any aid. It could take a week for the Army to arrive from Fort Buchanan, McLane, or Fillmore. They were on their own. Butterfield had armed them with Sharp's breech-loading rifles that took a paper cartridge. The rising breech-block snipped off the end of the paper to expose the powder. It still had to be capped but could fire three times as fast as a muzzle-loading musket with less exposure to the shooter and with two or three times the range. Each man also had two of Colt's revolving pistols. They had the firepower of ten times their number, but the Apache outnumbered 500 to 1.

Not one to take chances, Butterfield also made gifts to the Apache on their promise that his stages would pass their country unmolested, and his station-keepers hired them to gather firewood and hay, two tasks that would have meant great exposure to the men away from the station.

"Hallo, the station!" I cried. "Put a stranger up till morning. I'll cut firewood for you."

Not so much a stranger perhaps, I'd met Joseph, so the station-keeper was called, in Mesilla. Young, tall, and well-framed, he was one of many young men who'd come west from New York with Butterfield where he, Butterfield, had run a stage line. He wore simple work clothes with an incongruous black top hat. His mates were similarly clothed but wore wide brimmed, Mexican straw hats. A station-keeper and two hostlers were the usual complement at these lonely stations. At some stations, there was a relief driver as well, for the stage ran day and night in order to cover the miles from St. Louis to San Francisco in only twenty-eight days.

The drivers knew their section of road so well they could drive it in the dark. They drove 100 miles or so and then switched out. They'd return the way they'd come with the next stage from the other direction. It was all part of running at nine-miles-per-hour day and night in dark or light.

"Howdy, Bray." Joseph called back. "We've been expecting you, and I sent the word down the line that you'd be coming. The station-keepers will be glad of your company if you'll share the news and gossip. The drivers will welcome an outrider."

I'd given my name as Bray from St. Gnomebray. It was close enough to the name with which my sainted mother had blessed me.

"Surely," I said dismounting, "you Butterfields have got the latest news from the States before anyone else."

"Aye," he smiled, "but hearing the same mouths tell it over and again becomes tiresome very quickly."

Dinner was a stew of uncertain parentage prepared by one of the hostlers. It looked odd but smelled good enough, or perhaps I was just hungry. Fortunately salt and chili were plentiful. The biscuits hadn't risen as they should and remained doughy; perhaps the saleratus was spoilt. The coffee was strong, and there was plenty of sugar.

After dinner, cards came out and a bottle of Mexican cactus liquor, *tequila.* We passed the bottle around. It was the only alcohol readily available although its taste and smell seemed oddly astringent and mildly unpleasant like the cactus themselves. Joe produced a fiddle and began to torture it until the cries of those assembled forced him to stop.

"Dang," said one of the hostlers; I've forgotten his name, "wish we had a Mexican gal to entertain us and cook."

"Or even a squaw," said the other.

Joe grimaced. "Yeah, but I wouldn't let her cook."

"And maybe you could learn to sing," said the first hostler, "or, dare I say it, learn to play the fiddle."

For a moment, seeing the look on Joe's face, I thought he'd soon be placing an advert for a new hostler. The moment passed quickly. These men had to be easy going to survive long at these lonely stations.

We passed the evening in talk and cards and retired early.

"You can sleep here," said Joe indicating a spot in one of the two rooms that were roofed. "Long as you promise not to snore. With four of us in the room, it gets pretty tight."

"You sure you want him inside?" demanded an hostler overhearing Joe's invitation to me. "Just this October, the staff at Dragoon Springs was murdered in their sleep." Then he grinned. "Guess we can take the risk if Joe will stay up to watch him."

Nonetheless, it was gracious of them to let me sleep inside the station house. Although the station was sixty by sixty feet with a ten-foot-high wall, only two ten by ten rooms had roofs. The remaining area was open for stabling. With the stock inside the walls, Apaches were less likely to steal it or attack. One room was for storage, the other for sleeping. It was crowded.

Ignoring the hostler, Joe went on. "Coach should be here tomorrow afternoon."

An *horno* in the corner kept the room warm long after the fire had died away.

I worked through the day earning my board and keep and departed with the stage in the afternoon. The driver was happy to have me as an outrider on my strawberry roan saddle horse. I tied my mule on behind the stage.

"Yup," the driver called down, spitting tobacco juice, "no stagecoach been attacked by Patches on this stretch. Gonna be a day though. Mark my words. Ole Mangas Coloradas gonna attack an' roast us all over a low fire!" He spat again for luck.

There were only two passengers. I could understand why. The fare from St. Louis to San Francisco was $200! Nobody had that kind of money. Butterfield carried mail and didn't care much for passengers, one of which called out to me.

"Trade you places! Let me ride the horse. You can have my comfortable seat."

"Think not," I replied. "I've heard the only way to survive in that coach is to stay drunk all the way to the Golden Gate."

"I'm workin' on it," he called back.

We rode toward the sunset with me keeping ahead or off to one side to stay out of the dust. I figured my well-fed horse was good for sixty miles at the pace the stage set. The stage changed horses at Rough & Ready and again at Good Sight. Each time, I wiped sweat from the roan, unsaddling him to let him rest a little. I fed corn and oats to the mule and the roan and watered them while bathed in the reek of horse sweat and saddle leather. I checked their legs and hoofs. They were doing well. I was as dark as an

Apache, covered with dust, and couldn't close my jaws without hearing them grind on trail grit. My legs and hindquarters were sore.

By the time we reached Cooke's Spring, I could hardly stand but watered and fed my stock while the stage exchanged horses.

The conductor climbed down from his box and paced about nervously holding his rifle at port arms, ready for trouble. "I don't like this place," he shared. "Cooke's Spring, Doubtful Canyon, and Apache Pass, all prime spots for an ambush!"

"I hear the Apache leave you alone," I replied.

"First time for everything," he grimaced. "We make the passengers carry guns because we're cautious. The day will come. Mark my words. Apache may be civil for now, but they're not friendly. Not by a long chalk. Ol' Mangas Coloradas don't like havin' us in his country. Something will set him off, and there ain't enough troops to protect us." It did, and there weren't, but Apache war was still a few years away.

I'd heard of Mangas Coloradas, Red Sleeves. Stories said his arms were red with the blood of his enemies. He was a big man, one of the biggest, said to be six foot and four inches. He ruled the roost and owned the mountains north and south of Butterfield's trail from Mesilla to Doubtful Canyon. The land from Doubtful Canyon to the San Pedro belonged to his son-in-law, Cochise.

I said that he climbed down from his box as if he'd been on a huge Concord stagecoach, but Butterfield didn't use the huge, heavy Concord stagecoaches. He'd designed the Celerity wagon with canvas top and sides. It had a flat, board floor 42 inches wide with three seats on the same level. The first two faced front and back. Driver and conductor sat up front with passengers behind them. The middle seat was the same. Only 42 inches wide, when three passengers sat abreast, those on the outside dangled their legs outside the coach. Inside they sat with their knees interlocked. At night, the seat backs folded down to make a flat bed and the passengers slept, or tried to, on top of each other. They didn't get much sleep or anything else. They had fifteen minute stops for food and outhouse.

Asleep in the saddle most of the way, I don't remember the stretch to Mimbres Crossing. I was barely able to unsaddle my horse and unpack the mule as the sun came up. Hobbling the stock, I set them to graze and sought a shady spot away from the station for myself glad, that the next westbound stage wasn't due for more than three days.

We, the stock and I, rested at Mimbres Crossing until the stage came and then repeated the trip from Picacho passing Ojo de Vaca, Soldier's Farewell, and Barney's and stopping at Stein's the gateway to Doubtful Canyon. I rode in daylight and saw more of the country, a wide prairie with high mountains to the north and small ranges, scarcely more than hills, scattered to the south. Peaks visible at great distance were sentinels for each of the stations. Shaped like a pyramid Stein's Peak, for instance, was easily recognizable. *Peloncillo* the Mexicans called it, a sugar cone or maybe little baldy, the two words are similar and both apply.

The ride across the Animas Playa was smooth but the dust was especially fine, like the silt that gathered at the bottoms of dry lakes. I had to tie a bandana across my face, and even so, the grit still got into my eyes.

There was a story about this country, specifically about Soldier's Farewell. When Major Steen led four companies of dragoons across the desert to take possession of Tucson, he stopped at the spring at Soldier's Farewell. That night, a dragoon went around the camp shaking hands with all his friends and acquaintances and bidding them "farewell." When he'd completed his rounds, he stuck his horse pistol in his mouth and blew his brains out the back of his head. He'd made a proper soldier's farewell. The country has that effect on some people. I wondered if I'd be one of them. Would I, failing to find my fortune in this desolate land, decide to take my own life? There were rumors about the young soldier. Some said he had a letter from his sweetheart saying she wasn't waiting any longer and was getting married. If so, he must have kept it with him quite some time, carrying it all the way from Santa Fe. So, it must have been the country getting to him. No woman could hurt a man that bad, I thought. How could a man get that lonely for a woman? It was the countryside.

The land was brown this time of year, and the playas, shallow lakes west of Barney's, were dry. It looked as though the road might be underwater for miles during the summer rains.

Stein's was not as pleasant as Mimbres Crossing. The station was of stone and fortified and far from help and human habitation.

The station-keeper talked of how the stations got their names. "Stein's Peak ought to be spelled s-t-e-e-n, Steen's, and pronounced that way to, for Major Steen who brought the dragoons to Tucson two years past. It's named for him. That same trip gave us Soldier's Farewell. You'd think it was where military escort turned back, but it ain't.

"One of Captain Ewell's men," he continued, "went kind of crazy, figuring he'd come to the very end of the world and didn't want to go no further. So, he went around telling everyone 'farewell.' When he'd told them all goodbye, he blew his own brains out with a big pistol." He grinned at his presumed wit. He knew, and the way he told the story showed it, no woman could affect a man like that. It was the place for sure.

"That would place us two stations beyond the end of the world," I frowned.

He cackled in response and proceeded to tell me how Mexicans that used this trail as their road from Santa Fe to Sonora had named this spring Ojo de Vaca, Cow Springs.

Doubtful Canyon was everything that its name implied. From both east and west entrances, it was difficult to detect. The Apache raided here so often that it was doubtful a traveler would get through. The road ran uphill between Stein's Peak and the Peloncillo Mountains for a few miles and then dropped suddenly into the west canyon whose walls close in until there is scarcely room enough for the stage to pass. Apache Pass wasn't much better. Ewell's was in the open valley near another dusty playa, the area home to millions of cranes who flew in clouds across the sky and settled by their thousands carpeting the plain to eat.

I arrived at Dragoon Springs at daybreak and after tending my stock, fell into a deep sleep. I dreamed of fair, *piskie* maidens, fine of form and loving but crazy in their ways leading a man to ruination and the country ahead was full of them. Long red hair floated in clouds behind them.

Chapter 5 - Dragoon

I awoke to a voice loudly demanding, "Who in hell is that?"

Tilting back the sombrero that had shaded my eyes from the morning sun, I beheld an officer in a blue uniform with orange facings, wearing a hat like a flower pot with an orange bud on top. He's a dragoon then, I told myself. Boots with spurs high enough to protect his shins and knees indicated an officer with at least some sense of "field duty." A rattling saber and Colt's revolver hung at his sides. A huge mustache groomed in fine Prussian fashion completed the costume. He's a boy, I thought, trying to look older.

"*Sin nombre*," I mumbled under my breath very much wanting him to let me continue my rest. "*Hombre Sin Nombre*."

"What the devil sort of name is that?" The young lieutenant was still trying to convince the men how tough he was by his manner of speech. This one could take lessons from my old commander, Captain Richard Ewell, who rarely raised his high pitched voice but was the bravest man alive, and Company G, 1st Dragoons, knew it.

"Anglo-French like Sinclair, Saint Claire," I replied. "In this case, Saint Gnomebray, g-n-o-m-e-b-r-a-y, but the *g* is silent. He was a Celtic saint, but no one remembers his name, except my family. The church didn't like him carrying on with the 'little people,' the gnomes and the *piskies*, uh, pixies." I corrected myself. "Owen Bray." I pronounced it very distinctly. "My friends call me Bray."

Not bad, I thought, for just coming out of deep slumber.

Behind him I heard a guffaw that strangled into a cough as a kerchief hid what might have been a smile on a captain of below average height. His blue "mushroom cap" came off and the kerchief moved up to wipe a head his men would soon immortalize by naming a peak for it, Mount Baldy. I pulled the sombrero back over my features, hoping he hadn't seen me, for this was Captain Richard Ewell, hisself.

"What are you doing here, Mr. St. Gnomebray?" the lieutenant demanded.

"Trying to get some sleep after a hard ride," I responded.

His men snickered and the lieutenant realizing that this conversation was apt to lead to further embarrassment broke off the pursuit.

Distant cries drew our attention to the dragoons' horse herd. I rolled onto my stomach and looked south toward the mountains named for Company G, the Dragoon Mountains. A detail had apparently taken the horses to the mouth of the canyon a quarter of a mile away to water at the spring. A huge black animal with horns the width of an oxbow charged the herders who boldly tried to fend it off. Again and again the creature charged.

"What in the world is that?" I exclaimed to no one in particular.

"Wild bull," a soldier replied.

The man I'd met as station keeper for Dragoon Springs the night before chimed in. "Feral bull. Mexicans tried to ranch here thirty years ago, but the Apache made them give it up. Killed most of 'em, the Mexicans, that is. They let their stock go wild and left. The stock flourished and is all over the valley now. The cattle are wild, *cimarron*, and unmanageable. The bulls attack everything. Even drove off Colonel Cooke's Mormon Battalion in the late war. I hear it was the only battle in which American forces was defeated."

The huge black creature, covered in scars, boasted more muscle than I'd ever seen on a bull. His eyes seemed to glow red. A cloud burst from his nostrils when he snorted, probably dust, but I swear it was fire, and his hooves sparked on the stony ground like steel on flint. I learned later that the herd was doomed. The Apache liked the meat of cows and hunted them, the result being that there were too many bulls and not enough cows. The bulls were sexually frustrated and had gone mean, real mean. They were longhorn Mexican stock that pretty much took care of themselves on the range, even ran off predators. All a stockman had to do was trim most of the yearling bulls and let them roam as steers. But they were mean in their current state.

The bulls might be difficult to handle, but there had to be some cows and calves out there and I saw the door to my future opening. The Army and the mines had to need beef in this country. I could supply it. I'd be rich. Here was beef I could herd, beef I didn't need to buy. I shouldn't need to be a reiver, a rustler, to find my cows.

"Why don't they shoot the thing?" I asked.

"Just makes 'em mad," someone said.

"That's where the Mormons went wrong," said the station keeper.

A man I'd met when I was in Company G, who ranched up near Fort Massachusetts and the Spanish Peaks, told me how he'd herded buffalo, gentling them by capturing cows and calves in a box canyon. When the calves grew, they were gentle and used to his presence. If a man could gentle and domesticate buffalo, I was sure I could do it with feral cattle.

The engagement continued until, satisfied he'd won, the bull broke it off.

My prospects were looking up. I saw a route to wealth and position. But would I find love or become old and mean like these bulls? Ah well, there were always casual loves, girls you could marry for an evening. It wasn't completely satisfying but kept a man from going mean.

Hoping I hadn't been recognized, I availed myself of this opportunity to water my stock at the spring some distance away, trying to keep the station between Captain Ewell and myself. The station was of stone laid in adobe mortar ten feet high and about sixty by forty feet around. Except for two small rooms, the interior was open to the sky.

As I passed around the back, I heard voices from inside, one of them quite high pitched and well known to me.

"Lieutenant, let the men rest but be ready to ride within the hour," said Captain Ewell. "The raiders we're following don't seem to have come this way. We'll head south along the western slope of the mountains."

"Yes, sir."

The captain belched his strange laugh again and choked it off.

"Sir?"

"The man you met," the captain said.

"Yes, sir, Mr. Owen Bray St. Gnomebray," Lieutenant Lord replied. "What about him, sir?"

"Don't you speak any Spanish yet, lieutenant?" Captain Ewell queried.

"Some, sir."

"The man told you his name was Hombre Sin Nombre," said Ewell choking on his strange laugh.

"Sir?"

"He told you he was a Man with No Name!" The laugh came again. "I knew him by another name when he served as a sergeant in Company G."

"He must be on the dodge, sir!" the lieutenant exploded finally understanding the captain's mirth. "Shall I have the men bring him in?"

"No, we'll respect his privacy," said Captain Ewell. "He was a first rate soldier when I knew him."

I took my time with the stock, returning after the dragoons had departed and then going west to the San Pedro River and south toward a range of mountains called Huachuca. It was always best to follow water in this country. I needed to find water in a canyon with a narrow mouth and steep sides. I'd soon trap some cattle.

Chapter 6 - A New Home

Heading south up the San Pedro Valley, the river is one of those few that flows north, I saw plenty of feral cattle and wondered why the Apache didn't hunt them. They had no aversion to beef, rustling beeves from Mexican and American alike. They rustled so much beef, as well as horses and mules, which they ate, rather than rode, I had to wonder if they still hunted wild game. The wild bulls were dangerous, charging whenever I drew close to their herds and even when they caught my smell. The long horns would have made them difficult prey for men on horse or foot armed only with lance or bow and arrow, I thought.

My requirements for a place were complex. I needed a valley with a narrow mouth. Unfortunately, there were no riverside cliffs here to form an enclosure. It would have to have water and good grass, and it needed to be away from Apache raiding trails and in a spot where I could disguise my smoke. If the Apache came, I'd try to trade or give them some beef, but I preferred they not know I was there. For my house I'd need a place not easily seen where trees would break up my chimney smoke so that it wouldn't be outlined against the sky. I'd also need good fields of fire for my guns where Apache and bandits couldn't approach me from behind, a cave or a place against a cliff, perhaps.

I finally found a valley with good grass, a flowing stream, and sides steep enough to discourage cattle from wandering. I blocked escape routes with twists of brush and fallen trees not wanting to build fences obvious to the Apache. A quarter mile of open ground among trees needed to be closed up at the entrance, and I set to work. In a side canyon, against a cliff above the valley floor, I found a place for my home and built it using native rock and mud for mortar. Two stories high, I built it, with my stable for my riding stock and tack room on the first level and a place to live above that. Only the entrance hatch from below would have to be defended in a fight.

Apache aren't foolish about losing men in a fight. They seek easy targets, for they're out for gain and not for glory.

Once other arrangements were ready, I needed a cow in milk. I'd have to risk the habitations of men. Apart from Captain Ewell, who'd already recognized me and was keeping my secret, I thought the chances of being recognized small, and besides, I'd come to the ends of the earth. I was beyond Mesilla and 300 miles beyond law and order in a land where the devil was on the loose. If I wanted to sell beef to the Army, I'd have to talk to Ewell.

I rode north to the Babocomari River and followed it west until I was in sight of Sonoita Creek. I found Fort Buchanan on a hillside above a swampy bottomland near the head of Sonoita Creek with water on three sides. It was the strangest post I'd ever seen with buildings scattered here and there as if a drunk had laid out the street plan. I learned later that it may have been so. The enlisted men were on their own when they came to the site Captain Ewell had selected. Ewell was away on other duties and they were tired from the long march. His site was on the mesa above, but they didn't want to carry water that far. When he arrived, the post was already constructed. Even in this dry season, I saw this was a marshy area. It was all mud huts in no particular pattern, no company streets. The buildings were scattered as though someone had dropped them there by accident; they were near low ground, too.

The milk cow wasn't for me. I hoped to stake her out and attract a few calves. Maverick's would certainly come and maybe others. It was free milk. And from this start I could build a herd.

Hobbling my horse and turning him out on good grazing, I lurked in the shadows awaiting a chance to talk to Captain Ewell.

"Ah, sergeant," he said as I approached, "I wondered when you'd turn up."

"Sergeant no more, captain," I replied. "Now I run cattle, or hope to, and hunt a little when there's time."

"And I suppose you're looking for a market," Ewell replied.

"Aye, sir, I am."

The short, bald officer didn't have to consider this proposition for long. "We'll take your cattle, though you'll have competition from ranches and farms on Sonoita Creek. My officers will be happy of game for the table. I have a mine with some of the other officers some miles south of here. We call it Patagonia." He explained how to get there following a creek southeast for 12 miles from where it joined Sonoita Creek. "The miners will want beef and game as well as will Sarah Bowman, the Great Western, who runs a house near there."

"Not the tall, red-haired wench we knew in Mexico?" I asked.

He smiled. "The same. Hero of Fort Brown and favorite of General Taylor."

"Her presence alone might make the trip worthwhile," I responded.

"Remember Paddy Graydon?" Ewell asked.

"The scheming Irish corporal?" I responded.

"He took his leave of the service and runs a house of ill-repute, the Boundary Hotel, not three miles from here."

I stayed the night with Ewell, sharing the dinner he offered.

"Tell me, sir," I queried, "why did someone pick this spot for a fort?"

"I selected it," he said a little piqued. "The grass and water are good for our horses. The low ground keeps off the wind, and we're not going to defend this position, so we don't need a fortification. You should see the company garden!" He looked down for a moment, a sign of embarrassment, and mumbled, "I had intended that it be built a little higher on the mesa."

Ewell was famous for his company gardens. He grew them well, producing surplus that led to a company fund of almost $2,000, or so I had been told. The men of Company G, 1st Dragoon Regiment, lived well as a result.

"Ah," he sighed, "I think I'll return home, leaving the service to become a gentleman farmer and take myself a wife as well."

I heard from others that there was trouble with Swamp Fever at Fort Buchanan in the wet summer months, and the Captain Ewell always arranged to be away when the rains came.

Riding south along Sonoita Creek, I encountered a farmer named Grundy who had a cow in milk. I arranged to buy it and pick it up on my return. Following the stage road, I crossed the Santa Rita Mountains, passing the Hacienda Santa Rita and mines and arriving in hot, low country along the Santa Cruz River at Tubac. Tubac was the hub of mining activity in what was coming to be called Arizona, although it was still New Mexico Territory. The town was a collection of adobe buildings along two narrow streets. A collapsing presidio dominated the town. The mining company for its own use had restored parts of it. Tubac was a town with a blacksmith and a store or two. It was where I needed to come to purchase supplies. Tucson was my other choice, but it had an unsavory reputation as refuge for men on the dodge from California committees of vigilance and Judge Lynch.

A voice called to me from the shadow of an adobe wall. "*Señor*, give a poor soul some tequila, *por favor*."

Needing information, I purchased a bottle and took it back to my new acquaintance. Tall and thin, emaciated, he was dressed in rags and beaded buckskin with a large straw sombrero. His left leg was not straight and I guessed he walked only with difficulty. High cheek bones and his dress suggested that he was not just an Indian, but also an Apache. However, many Mexicans dressed in cotton rags, so Juan did not stand out as not being one of them.

Sitting beside him, I handed him the bottle. "Who are you, *amigo*, and who are your people?" I asked in as kindly a manner as I could manage. I lit my nose-warmer and after a few puffs, handed it to him. He drank, handed the bottle back, and puffed.

Blowing smoke, he replied, "*Gracias, señor*, I am called Juan Largo, and I am of the *Indeh*. Do you know what this means?"

"The people," I replied. "Apache."

"*Si*," he continued. "Apaches related to the *Pinaleños*, but now we are called Apache *Mansos*, the tame ones. When my grandfather was young, the Spanish asked us to become soldiers to defend them from the Apache. They paid us well. The Mexicans not so well."

I handed him the bottle and then the pipe to encourage him to continue.

"Since the Americanos have come," he continued, "we have nothing, and we are wretched. Once we ruled all the country from the Santa Ritas east to the San Pedro River. This was our territory, and we fought the Chiricahua. We allied with the Sopaiburi against them, trading with these farmers for corn, giving them salt and game. The Chiricahua still avoid our country and do not live there. They know it is our land, but they hate us and our cousins the *Pinaleños*. Now we are *mansos,* and we are wretched." He fell silent. Mourning the descent of his people, I thought.

Leaving him with the bottle and pipe, I went to find him some food, thinking myself lucky. My new home in the Huachucas was not home to Apaches. It was a no-man's land between the holdings of various bands and that suited my purposes. They raided in this prime country but did not live here. Returning with tortillas, carne asada, and refritos, I came around the corner of a building and promptly jumped back into the shadows. There in the street stood O'Malley and with him was a large man I knew must be Jacko Helligan from his size and demeanor. I presumed the rest of the gang was nearby.

Fortunately, I remained unseen and made my way back to my spot in the shadows with the *viejo manco*, the old cripple, my Apache *manso* friend.

"*El hombre* is *muy malo*, a very bad man," he said unbidden. I hadn't thought he'd seen Helligan or my near encounter. This Apache was more alert than I realized. "Last night he murdered a man who accused him of cheating at cards. But there is no *alcalde* and no soldiers to arrest him. No one is brave enough. Señor Poston talks big, but he is not so brave, I think. Nor so foolish." He grinned. "So bad men walk the *camino* and do as they wish."

"So," I said in sympathy, "times are bad since the Americanos have come. The bad men are free to make more trouble than before."

"It is the same," he replied. "But Americano bad men are bigger, stronger, and better armed."

We continued talking companionably in the shade all afternoon. He proved a wealth of knowledge about the country, its plants, animals, and people and shared this with me as he drank my wine and puffed my nose-warmer.

Chapter 7 - Avoiding Trouble

We watched as O'Malley, Jacko Helligan, and most of their crew rode out of town to the north. I bid Juan Largo *buenos dias*, knowing I would look him up again. He was a valuable man, one who observed and retained information. Seeking dinner in a tiny café, I found myself sharing a table with Charlie Poston, a fine looking man of medium height whose eyes darted while he considered what he would say. While not ostentatious, his clothing was clean and neat, making him stand out in this Arizona country.

"My mines are going well. There's incredible wealth here," Poston said. "The soil is rich and the climate warm. Farmers can bring in two or even three crops a year. Imagine!"

"Looks a bit dry," I replied.

"The river! We'll irrigate," Charlie said. "Indians have been doing it for centuries. Jesuits taught them how, no doubt."

"Where are the Jesuits?" I asked.

"They were all Germans and north Italians, same thing." He smiled. "Spanish decided they didn't trust 'em in 1767 and drove them all out. Replaced 'em with Franciscans."

"So where are the Franciscans?" I asked, although I already knew. You couldn't be in New Mexico long without noticing the shortage of priests.

"They were all Spaniards," Poston said. "After independence from Spain, Mexico didn't trust them anymore and drove them out."

"Who performs weddings and such?" I asked.

"Why, I do. It's how I keep my workers. I told them under American law as *alcalde* I could perform weddings and funerals and such," Poston grinned. "I do for free that for which the church used to charge three month's salary."

"Is that legal?" I asked.

Poston grinned. "It works, and it keeps them happier than they've ever been." He changed the subject. "As there is no *la fonda*, no inn, here in Tubac as yet, you're welcome to stay with me at the Sonoran Mining and Exploration Company offices."

"I appreciate that," I said extending my hand receiving his in return. I'd count my fingers later in private. With this one, they'd slip away, and I wouldn't even notice. We walked to his residence.

As the night wore on, we drank from his bottle, and I listened to his talk of the prospects of his mines, his company, Arizona, and Sonora. Apparently he had it in mind that the Sonora should soon be part of the United States. "It's the seaports. They're not far off. Less than 200 miles," he rambled. "We could easily ship gold and silver from here by sea and get the things we need in return. And a railroad, we'll soon have that, too. The Butterfield Overland Mail is just the beginning."

I'd read his book, *Reconnaissance in Sonora*. He made a lot of claims, but there didn't seem to be much substance to them. He certainly seemed to believe everything he was saying about Sonora, or at least her ports, becoming part of the United States and the great wealth to be found underground. He was full of grand ideas and a natural salesman, but he couldn't quite meet your eye when he talked about his mines. There were indications that they weren't producing, as they ought, whispers of poor management. The man was a dreamer, a visionary. At least, that was my impression.

Late in the evening, he grew maudlin in his cups and wept for the family he'd left behind somewhere. He had a wife and children. There'd been dreams there, too, but they hadn't worked out either, so he'd come west to fresh dreams. In San Francisco, he'd made some money as customs inspector, thought he had the connections, and saw his chance in Sonora. His tale was not uncommon, but he did seem to have managed it on a grand scale.

Near midnight as I was looking for an excuse to retire, we heard shots from down the street. I leapt to my feet and armed myself, checking the loads on my pistols and feeling for my knife. Poston remained seated.

"There's nothing to be done," he mumbled. "It's just Jacko Helligan's men, and they don't bother my mining company."

"What do you suppose they're doing?" I asked, incredulous at his words.

"Oh, killing a Mexican for sport," he said, "or recovering their money from someone fool enough to beat them at cards."

"Aren't you the law?" I stared at him. "The *alcalde*. In New Mexico the *alcalde* is judge, sheriff, mayor, and commander of the militia all in one."

"Technically, I'm only a justice of the peace," he replied. "The nearest court is in Santa Fe. Even if I made an arrest, there's no way to get them tried."

"So you won't do anything?" I was stunned.

"Perhaps we could elect a marshal . . ."

I walked stiffly through the door and then, clinging to the shadows, moved up the street. The commotion was dying down. Sounds came from an adobe *sala*, a gambling parlor. Juan Largo's voice called to me from deep shadow where he sat leaning against the wall, listening.

"They shot the stranger. They made him join their game. When he won, they shot him," Juan said. "He's inside. Now, they say they will let him bleed to death."

I looked through the open doorway only partially covered by a blanket. Light for the interior came from a single lantern under a low blackened ceiling, in a room filled with smoke. There were a few tables with chairs but most of the Mexicans within sat on the floor. Americans took the few chairs available. A man lay doubled with pain bleeding on the floor as four men sat at a table laughing, drinking, and playing cards. The others within seemed terrified into immobility.

Without thinking - if I'd thought I wouldn't have done it - I tied my bandana over my face and pulled my broad-brimmed flat-crowned straw sombrero low over my face. Pulling and cocking my pistols, I stepped to the doorway keeping to the exterior shadows.

Speaking to the seated men, I ordered, "Hands flat on the table. Move and I shoot. Señorita," I motioned to a girl. "*Por favor*. Take their guns and put them in his hat." She pulled a hat off one of the men, extracted their weapons, and placed them into the hat. "Good, now take all the money on the table and put it in the hat, too."

"Hey, you can't do that!" the hatless man yelled. "That's robbery!"

I fired into the table next to his hand, the flash and flame bright in the room, the noise deafening. The haze in the room grew thicker and more acrid. There was no point in saying anything. A dragoon colt had spoken my lines.

"Outside," I ordered. "Get on your horses and ride and don't come back. If I see you, I'll shoot you on sight."

They rode. I stepped into the shadows and waited.

Not five minutes had passed before the thunder of hoof beats approached from the darkness beyond town, a single horse coming at high speed. The rider crouched low in the saddle clinging to a rifle.

When he was two lengths from me, I stepped from the shadows and fired into his passing forehead so close his hair caught fire. The horse reared, and he tumbled off. There was no need to check; he was dead.

Stepping into the *sala*, I said, "Help him." A man rose, and the *señorita* who had helped with the hat joined him. Together they assisted the groaning wounded man to his feet. "Take him to *el jefe* Poston."

I gathered up the hat still full of money and guns and followed after the three into the night. I was alert for danger. The señorita stumbled on the fresh corpse in the dark. "Watch your step," I whispered helpfully.

"Poston," I said as we entered his office-home, "do you have a doctor."

"I usually . . ." he stuttered.

"Then help the man," I said flatly in a voice that didn't brook disobedience. I dumped the hat on his table. "I'll be taking my leave now. Thanks for your hospitality. *Howsumever*, the *capperause* up the street got *oogly,* and I've laid one of Helligan's devils low, and it'll be *kicklish* for me to show my face hereabouts for a while."

"You can't leave me with this mess!" he roared.

"It's your town and welcome to it," I almost smiled and then realized it was best not to insult him. I needed his friendship. "I doubt they'll associate me with you. They didn't get much of a look at me. I'm just a passing highwayman.

"Charles," I continued, "look after this man. Patch him up and hide him. I'm afraid they'll take revenge out on him."

Poston nodded. Despite bluster and boosterism, there was a reasonably good, if self-centered man, somewhere down deep. "I'll take him to Tumacacori. It's an old mission church. A blacksmith works there and he's been our nurse before."

Accepting that Poston would care for the wounded man, I saddled my horse, loaded my mule, and rode east into the darkness across the Santa Cruz River on the stage road to Fort Buchanan and the Patagonia Mine.

The first part of the journey across the river plain was easy. I planned to pick a likely spot when I came to the mountains and set up in some rocks with a view of the trail. If they came after me, I'd ambush them, but I thought it would be a while. They didn't have guns, and by the time they figured out Poston had them or retrieved guns from their friends, I'd be well up in the mountains. The mountains were rough, the trail cut by deep canyons and arroyos. I was surprised a stage came this way. Certainly it couldn't carry much of a load. It was probably just a buckboard that carried mail from the fort and mines.

Chapter 8 - Looking for Love in all the Wrong Places

Outside town in the deep dark, I finally removed my bandana mask. Then, carefully and by feel alone, I reloaded my dragoon colt. I had fired two cylinders; one was still under the hammer, the other just in advance of it. I fished my powder and poured while the horse followed the eastbound trail without help from me. I topped the cylinders' balls, rammed them home, and then lubricated the front of the cylinder to prevent chain-fire. Finally, I capped the cylinders. With my weapons ready again, I kicked the horse to a faster pace.

Riding at night is no easy matter, but the trail from Tubac to Hacienda Santa Rita, the mines, was clear even by starlight. Approaching the mountains, I found a place off the trail to rest. I was in the western lea of the peaks, and the sun was going to be late coming up from my prospective.

I arose late intending to take my breakfast at the Hacienda Santa Rita or in the Sonoita Valley, but found fresh tracks on the trail. I stopped and breakfasted from my saddlebags on jerked meat and stale tortillas while I considered this new information. They pursued me; of that I had no doubt. Were they tracking me and had missed my trail in the morning twilight? Were they waiting in ambush up ahead? Should I take a few days off at the Hacienda until, not finding a trail, they lost interest? What would I do if they came back? I opted to go cross-country, following Indian trails where I could, to Grundy's farm on Sonoita Creek. I'd pick up my cow and look less suspicious. What self-respecting highwayman would allow himself to be caught while leading a milk cow?

I could make good time by heading up canyon away from Sonoita Creek to Patagonia where Captain Ewell had his mines 12 miles or so to the south. His mines were close to the San Rafael Valley, the transition from mountain and canyon to flat prairie quite sudden and unexpected. On the other side lay the Canelo Hills, the Huachuca Mountains, and my rancho. The San Rafael was open and flat. An observer on high ground in the Canelo Hills or Patagonia Mountains could see a rider from miles away. The Apache avoided it for this reason and kept to the hills. Perhaps I should cross at night. For now, I was trying to make the Casa Blanca, Great Western's establishment near the mines, before dusk. I was looking forward to her cooking. In addition to her courage, General Taylor had preferred her cooking to that of any other chef.

Sarah Bowman, the Great Western, named for the largest passenger ship of the day, stood over six foot two with flame red hair. An Army wife, she'd come West with the regiment after the Mexican War where she'd made her fortune organizing laundresses and the officer's mess while offering other services. Brave, smart, and wild, she was a favorite of General Taylor.

I was there when Mexican dragoons stalled Old Rough 'n' Ready's column.

As the colonels argued about what best to do, Sarah stomped up to the General and said, "Gen'l, loan me a pair 'o' britches, 'n' I'll go run 'em off myself!"

She meant it, too and likely would have done as much, if in her display the colonels hadn't found their courage and determination. At the close of the war, a colonel told she could no longer travel with the regiment because she wasn't married. Recently widowed, for the third time, she trooped the line proclaiming that she had a $10,000 dowry and begging to know who'd marry her that very day.

Her establishment, in the Patagonia Mountains near Ewell's mines, provided some of the finest cooking and other services then to be had in Arizona, as Doña Ana County, New Mexico Territory, was coming to be called. It took fortitude to maintain a lonely house with other women in Apache country. I expected she'd taught them to defend themselves. Nonetheless, even Poston feared Apache and bandito raids that swept right through Tubac.

I approached after dark. Light leaked around shuttered windows and doors. Six horses were tied up out front. "Men up from the mines," I thought. Casa Blanca was a small, adobe fortress, sighted with an eye to defense. There were no windows on the sides, only at the front and rear *portals*, recessed porches. The roof above the second story was crenelated like a castle. Tying my mules and cow around the back, I walked to the front, noticing murder holes above doors and windows as I entered. Even before I opened the door, the delightful aroma of Sarah's cooking, chilis, roasted beef, onion, and garlic, enveloped me.

Drawing wide the door, I was stopped cold by the tableau within the dining room. A man holding a partially clothed, whimpering girl to a tabletop was just starting to carve something into her chest with a bowie knife. I recognized the dissatisfied customer as a companion of the man I'd killed in Tubac. Sarah would never allow this, I thought. Then I saw her across the room with a knife at her throat. The man holding her arm was below average height; undoubtedly his friends, if any, would have christened him

"Shorty." His knife tip barely touched the red-haired Amazon's neck.

Looking up, the man with the girl roared, "Get out!"

That was all the distraction Sarah needed. She whirled and smashed her man in the nose with an elbow. As this sensitive organ spouted blood, she went to work on the rest of him. I was too busy to take precise notice of how. Taking one long step closer, the barrel of my Hawken rifle rose swiftly to bash the knifeman in the teeth. He dropped like a felled tree, and I thought we'd won the day.

A blow to the head from behind propelled me to my knees in agony; my vision narrowed and blurred. When it cleared a little, I found myself between two strong men whose vice-like grips pinioned my arms. Another pistolero held Great Western at gunpoint while our two victims slowly recovered on the floor. A big man was approaching as he hitched up his pants. Beyond Sarah, women in states of partial undress wept or screamed and crowded the stairway from the upper floor. The girl I'd rescued was screaming.

"Hold him," ordered the big man, hitting me in the stomach. "We'll teach this miner a lesson."

More blows followed. I looked for a chance to break free, but after a few to the head and stomach, I was too addled to resist. I could only retreat mentally and endure the pain without letting it control me. I didn't give up but an opening never came. The brute was methodical.

The man I'd hit rose slowly, his mouth bleeding. Groaning, he must have decided to extract vengeance for he again grabbed the girl by her hair and pulled her in front of me.

"Turk, my turn," he mumbled in obvious pain. "Think the miner likes the girl." The beating stopped momentarily as the big man, Turk, stepped aside.

"Okay, Hell," said Turk.

So these were Hellyar and Turk Pellewe, cousins to the Helligans. And they thought I was a miner, unrecognized from Tubac. Thank heaven for small favors. They might only beat me instead of killing me slowly.

Holding her with his left by her hair, Hell mumbled through his damaged mouth, "Like her, huh? I fix!"

With that he began carving on her with his recovered knife. Then he dropped the screaming girl and slashed open my shirt drawing blood. Leaning back into my captors restraining arms, I kicked him as hard as I could where he'd feel it. He doubled over.

"No more!" ordered Sarah. "No more. You'll never be welcome here again!"

Turk grabbed his brother's knife hand to restrain him. Then pushing Hell aside and stepping over the weeping girl, he began to pummel me again.

"I said, no more!" roared Sarah. The threat of being cut off from the best meals and girls in Arizona was not to be taken lightly.

The big man looked over his shoulder at her. "Take him outside," Turk said.

The two who had my arms dragged me out the door. "What shall we do with him?" asked one.

Smash mouth, Hellyar, mumbled, "Bottomless pit."

The big man nodded as Shorty joined the group dragging me up the hillside.

"Here it is!"

Between an outcropping of rocks, a crevice showed blacker than night. A Spanish 'rat-hole' mine, I thought, as they lifted me and dumped me in. I slipped and fell a few feet, slid some more, and grabbed a handhold. I'd found a ledge about fifteen feet down and wedged myself in where I'd be out of sight even if they thought to drop a candle or torch down the hole.

"I didn't hear him hit bottom," came a voice from above the mineshaft.

"That's because it's bottomless, stupid," said Shorty.

"Yeah, he hasn't hit bottom yet," said Turk who must have been dumber than he looked.

"He's done," agreed Hellyar.

"Let's get out of here. Place gives me the creeps," said Shorty.

"My grandpa told me there were ghosts in places like this," said another.

I heard no more. They must have moved away. I was in pain but soon passed into the bliss of unconsciousness, broken only by dreams of screaming, women with bloody breasts.

Chapter 9 - In a Cavern in a Canyon

Light woke me. It came from above, penetrating the dark uncertainly. I couldn't see the sky. My eyes were swollen nearly shut. The light had a reddish haze, caused by blood from broken vessels in my eyes. Feeling around me, I learned my world dropped off into blackness on three sides. How far it dropped I couldn't tell beyond the reach of a hand, an arm, a foot. I pushed a pebble off to my side. It clicked and rolled and dropped a very long way striking walls and ledges again and again before continuing silently to inky depths.

My body ached. Knotted, bruised muscles in my arms limited my motion. My head spun, and I couldn't think clearly. Then I blacked out again. When I opened my eyes again, the pain in my ribs was unbearable. I was cold. The rock was leaching away my body's warmth and making me stiff.

I couldn't stand, but I did crawl feeling my way until I came to a drop-off. The pain grew intense, and blackness took me again. I may have been out for days, hours, or only moments. I had no way to gage.

When I came to, I knew I was in old Spanish workings, very old. I found the remains of a ladder carved from a single notched log. What little wood remained was soft and punky, little more than crumbs. The Jesuits had used Indians to work mines here. Eighty years earlier, in 1767, the Spanish drove out the Jesuits. The Spanish hadn't trusted the Austrian-German, educated men of the Society of Jesus who reported directly to the Pope and who presumably sent gold and silver that should have gone to the Spanish Crown to the Society and the Holy Father instead. The mines closed, and the Jesuits didn't share their secrets with the Franciscans who replaced them. The *barreteros*, Indian miners, and thc *tenateros*, porters who hauled ore out of the earth, did not care to share the secrets of the mines. They did not wish to be returned to abject slavery in the dark, so the mines were lost.

The Spanish, Jesuits included, used *el sistema del rato*, the rational system in mining which German engineers, the only trained mining engineers of the day, denigrated as "rat hole" mining. Spanish miners would follow a vein of quartz bearing *oro*, ore, breaking it out in chunks with heavy, 20 and 30-pound, iron bars. Hence the miners were *barreteros*, bar men. When the quartz was too hard for the bar, they lighted fires and got the rock red-hot before throwing water on it to make it crack. The mine was no bigger than the vein and went in all directions like a rat hole. Drops were seldom great -10, 20, 30 feet - but the mine might wind deep into the mountain or rise again from depth to peak.

Stepping off a drop in the dark could be fatal and would at least cause a broken limb. With twists and turns, light didn't penetrate far. From the top, the mine appeared to go endlessly straight down in blackness all the way to the infernal regions. It looked black and bottomless. Within it would be a maze, a rat hole, running in all directions up, down, and sideways. It would be any easy place to become lost forever.

I thought of those who'd dumped me here, glad that they were stupid and superstitious, glad they hadn't dropped me onto the floor at the Casa Blanca and worked on my arms, legs, and back with their feet. My injuries were bad enough. My ankle was sprained and swollen. My bruised arms and chest made it hard to move, and bruised and broken ribs made it hard to breathe and crawl. I'd recover, but how would I get out of this hole? That's when the pain took me again, and I thought no more.

Consciousness came slowly, and I awoke thirsty. Ore deposits occur where there are anomalies in the rock, and spring water follows the same route. The water might be hot, even super-heated, or it might be full of poison, but there would be water. I felt around and soon found a drip that seemed to be pure. I was near the surface but likely to die slowly almost in reach of it. I was growing feverish from my injuries.

I dreamed of red-haired angels flying down to succor me where I lay. They moved strangely in the dark, bringing light, carrying candles, and jerking awkwardly like marionettes on strings.

I awoke to find one mopping my fevered brow with a soft and gentle touch. The dream changed. Now the angel was a large, red-haired Amazon suspended on a rope still brushing my brow with her soft hand.

"There you are," she said. "We'll get you out. Sorry, it took so long. We didn't know where they had taken you. 'Bottomless Pit', they said. We didn't know what they meant."

I didn't know what the angelic Amazon (archangel?) meant. My wits were addled and confused. I felt the soft touch and knew I was in heaven. I'd died and, to my surprise, made it into paradise.

"Then one of girls saw the marks where they'd dragged you up the hill," the angel continued, grunting as she forced a rope under and around me, bringing the pain back. I must have passed out again. The agony of being dragged up out of the hole wakened me. A band of dark haired angels, assisted by my mule, hauled me on a rope from black Hades to the light of paradise. Mules in heaven? It was unthinkable, but here he was. Horses, maybe. Dogs, surely. But mules? Never!

Sarah told me that I slept for days. I don't remember being fed soup, but I wish I did, for the girls took it by turns resting my head on their breasts as they fed me. I dreamed of angels. They told me later I insisted I was in paradise. Perhaps I was. My first clear thought, days later, was of one of the girls thanking me for saving her *hermana,* her sister. She shucked her robes and climbed into bed with me. Painful as it was, her manner of thanks was welcome.

As the days passed, others came. I couldn't send them away. That would have been ungracious, ungentlemanly. Guadalupe, the girl who'd been cut, came one day showing me how well her scars were healing. Finally, Sarah Bowman herself arrived.

"The food has been wonderful, Sarah," I said. "I'm feeling stronger."

"Glad you're recovering," she said. "You pulled us out of a fix."

"You pulled me out of a rat-hole," I responded. "I wasn't much help."

"You distracted them," she said. "I know men. It would have gotten a lot worse if they hadn't had you to drag off." She slipped off her things and stood there tall and imposing, red haired, more impressive than any statue Michelangelo had contrived. She knew things, wonderful things beyond imagining. I was in paradise.

After finishing a fine meal, I departed a few days later as the sun was setting. Though her girls might be more than waitresses, Great Western served the best food in Arizona.

"You keep that girl on the roof alert," I said. "All the time. It's not just Apache you're watching for anymore. Helligan's men might come back."

"It's you they're after, Bray," she said. I'd explained my new name to her. They probably weren't looking for me here, but there was no reason to wave a red flag in front of them. "I've run them off, told them not to come back."

"You know their kind, Sarah," I said. "That will just be an incentive to them. You've got to be alert and ready to fight." It's strange country where every girl has a loaded rifle and two pistols at her bedside and a pretty girl sits on the roof with a rifle, watching.

Sarah started to bend to kiss me, and then realizing I was as tall as she was, straightened and encircled me in a hug that would have broken a lesser man. She smelled of spices, her hair of lilac. Soft, wonderful thing pressed tight against me.

"Careful, girl. I might not leave," I said mounting my horse and riding toward the dark. As I left, I called back, "At least, they didn't kill my cow."

I rode across the San Rafael in the dark reaching water in the Canelo Hills toward dawn. It was a good place with tree shade and fine grass. I'd bring my cattle here to graze.

Chapter 10 - Cow Dreams

In the gap between the Huachucas and the Mustang Mountains, the sun rose each morning misty-red above the distant Chiricahuas and set in the evenings over Mount Baldy, named for Captain Ewell, in the Santa Ritas, in fiery displays of raging glory. Sun-fire licked through evening clouds shredding them before burning them down to a single glowing ember to disappear for the night. Mist gathered over the *cienegas*, marshy lowlands, and mustangs grazed in the low dells leading from the Babocomari as it flowed east to the San Pedro. Near thc old Babocomari fort, or rancho, the river ran clear and good through thick brush. These places were dense with the little people, *piskies,* and other fairy folk. I'd seen Jack Harry's dancing lights many an evening. I avoided these places that gathered the *hag*, mist, especially toward *kindle teening*, twilight, not wishing to find myself ranked among the *piskey-led.* Me old gaffer had taught me well and my mother, too, of the things that one must know to avoid the wiles of the fairy folk.

The mountains north of the Babocomari were named for a herd of wild horses that grazed thereabouts. Able to block up a thicket here and there along the river so tight even the mustangs couldn't get through, I managed to surprise watering horses and trap them long enough to toss a loop around their necks. A rancher needs horses. Mounts need to feed and rest between hard rides. Ponies had differing gaits. Some had long smooth steps good for extended rides, others had shorter strides and could turn sharply to run down cattle, while others were for plow and wagon, and still others had no fear of charging into dense brush. I gathered in four horses that week and set to work gentling them to the saddle.

Some would say I'd broken them, but breaking is hard on man and horse. The broken horse has his will destroyed and is sullen, uncooperative. A gentled horse is a partner who cooperates with the rider and tries to give him what he wants. That horse uses his head and thinks ahead; it anticipates.

Creating a brush corral with rope and brush to hold my stock at the river bank, I enclosed 20 feet of river. The river was the perfect place for a man working alone to train riding stock. I roped a horse and snubbed her down to a stump to get the bridle over her head, then pulled her into the water, and leapt aboard as I'd seen the Jicarilla Apache do back in the Rio Arriba north of Santa Fe. She bucked and fought but was up to her chest in the water and had trouble moving. She tried to spin and kick her hind quarters high in the air, but the mare's protests were in vain and soon she was mine.

Although I was riding bareback, I seldom got thrown, and then the landing was soft, more or less. Horses tire rapidly in waist-deep water and learn the faster for it. Soon they will allow a man on their back without protest. Within a week, I had a small *ramuda* and was beginning to appreciate each horse's talents. I'd need someone to look after them and keep them fed and watered. Tall, lame Manso Apache Juan Largo might be up to it.

My plan was to capture wild, very wild, feral cattle that had run loose after the Mexicans had abandoned the Babocomari Land Grant years ago. The wild bulls had fought the Mormon Battalion in the Mexican War, the only

Mexican unit to win a battle. I would lead a milk cow I had purchased near maverick calves and let them latch-on.

Working the rolling country between the Huachucas and the Babocomari, I was able to locate cows and calves that had wandered out of sight of their bulls. Finding ones that the bulls wouldn't soon miss was important. Early in the operation, I captured two calves and was leading my milk cow while a stray cow followed my little herd. It was a proper fine day, and I whistled a Cornish tune as I rode up the draw only to find a *gaert banger* of a huge bull snorting fire and huffing smoke, *Tantarabobus*, Satan his own self, with horns longer than my horse and hooves striking sparks off the flinty ground. I dropped the leads on the calves but hung onto my cow; I was out of business without her. I spurred my mustang fiendishly. Thank the One *Abew,* she was fresh, and up to a run and that there weren't *arry a hinderment* to slow *ussen*, for the cow was no jumper.

That bull kept coming so close I could feel his hot breath on my back. I jerked my big Colt Walker from where its holster was cinched to the pommel. It was a horse-pistol too heavy to carry on my hip, so I let the horse wear the holster. If anything could take this monster down, it would be the Walker. But what if it jus' gave him the *tantrums*? Maybe as a last resort I'd shoot the evil brute . . . or perhaps in the extremity I'd shoot myself, and the horse, rather than see *ussen* carried down to the nether regions by the Beast. Three miles we ran before the *rumbustious* bull gave up the chase as a bad job. Horse, cow, and I ran another three just to be sure. The occasional run-ins I had with long-horned Mexican bulls, I did not want to repeat. Not only did I lose the calves I'd gathered, but I also was lucky to escape with my life. And the cow ran dry.

With a dry cow, a short vacation was in order while she and the mare that saved my life rested. It was time to visit Tubac and talk to Juan. I rode north to the Babocomari thinking to search out its headwaters as I made my way through the *wogmire*, marsh that I usually avoided. The headwaters must be very near those of Sonoita Creek and Fort Buchanan, too. They were and those of Cienega Creek as well.

Half a mile, no less, from the river I espied a fey though *ansum* creature bathing therein. A fine nimbus of strawberry-red hair encircled her head. I thought at first that it might be Sarah. Who else would dare this lonely place to bathe? But as I neared I saw the naked figure was too finely shaped and small to be my friend. This creature was elfin-thin and tiny. I spurred my horse ahead *piskie-led* and *fer* sure. Was I to be *dolly moppin'* with some *merrymaid*? I didn't see *arry* a fishy tail nor was this a salt sea.

The fairy disappeared as if 'twere some *buckaboo*, a ghost. Slowed by tangled brush, it took me some minutes to reach the stream, and when I did there was nothing there, no sign at all save a tiny footprint in the sand of the bank. I didn't try to follow. That way was madness. I wasn't one to pursue *fancical* maidens through the *hag* and *wogmire*. I turned my course to the west toward friends, sure the fairy had gone east toward . . . nothing. The nearest dwelling was Brunckow's mine, twenty miles and more beyond the San Pedro. No woman would make such a trip alone in Apache country save maybe a *fancical piskie* maid.

Lighting my nose-warmer to steady my nerves, I pushed my thoughts in new directions. The rancho needed building, Juan Largo needed hiring, and I was beginning to think there might be wealth to be had under Sarah

Bowman's Casa Blanca. It seemed likely that the Jesuits had abandoned the old Spanish mines before they played out. I shuddered, thinking of the black depths and twisted passages. And there were Tommy Knockers down below, more little people. As I'd heard it, it was possible to appease the Tommy Knockers with offerings. Leave them a bit of bread, cheese and meat, some tobacco, and a candle, and they might even help and protect a miner. Cross them, and death was swift and sure. If a miner was well with them, they'd warn him of danger by knocking on the rocks.

Chapter 11 - Came a Miner

I checked over my firearms again as I did every morning, ensuring that they were clean, oiled, primed, and ready. Percussion weapons are *kicklish* and must be cared for like babies. The powder can wet, and the cap can fall off or fail to fire. If the cap explodes, as it's supposed to, it can fall into the works and jam the turning of the cylinder. It's good to fire them every few days for practice and have everything about them clean, fresh, and oiled.

I carried two of Colt's Dragoon .44 revolvers. Sam Colt based the Dragoon pistol on the improvements Texas Ranger Samuel Walker encouraged him to make to his original revolving pistol, but at four pounds, they were a full pound lighter than my Walker Colt was. Most of the time, I let my horse carry the Walker looped to the saddle horn. Carried on the hip, the Walker would drag the trousers off a man. I was big. I could manage it, but few others could. Few could hold that big pistol steady at arm's length. I managed that too.

Usually, I carried the Dragoons. When I drew the Walker, I surprised many by hitting targets they thought only a rifle could reach. The range and accuracy were that of a rifle and the Walker used as many grains of powder. When I was away from my horse, I carried the Dragoons on my hips, one on each side in cut down, no flap, military holsters, and butt forward. A little leather thong kept them from falling out.

My rifle was a .50 caliber Hawken, the best made, and my well sharpened and oiled knife had a hilt-guard making it more suitable for fighting. One powder flask served all my weapons, its spout cut to 25 grains. One charge per cylinder loaded my Dragoons, and two charges loaded the Walker and the Hawken.

There were those who carried extra cylinders for their pistols, loaded and ready. That works well with the Remington where a single pull on a rod released the cylinder, but the Colt had to be taken apart. So I carried two and the Walker. It was a while before they were all empty, and in that while I hoped I'd have time to reload. In a jam, a single charge of 25 grains worked for the Walker and the Hawken. They weren't as powerful nor did they have their normal range, but they'd do close in. In a fight, there was no time for a patch. While you're fumbling to load up proper, the enemy has closed to where you didn't need all that accuracy and added range. That's why the Army used muskets and musketoons. They weren't as accurate as rifled weapons but they loaded up a lot faster.

We were traveling back from Tubac, and the finest bordello in Arizona was on the way. While I sat there at a table in the Casa Blanca, tall Sarah Bowman arrived bringing me coffee. Juan Largo had liked my idea, although all I could offer was room and board and a share of profits, if any, at the end of the season.

"Sarah," I said, "let's take a walk up your hillside."

She blushed like a maiden getting a marriage proposal, but I didn't have romance in mind at all.

"That cave," I went on, "that I was dumped in last time I was here . . ." She nodded. "I think it's an old Spanish mine."

As we walked, I noticed quartz hiding under a thick bed of piñon needles and oak leaves. It wasn't bull quartz, either. It was well streaked with mineral blossom, azurite, malachite, dark silver sulfide, and here and there, thin wires that might be gold. Glancing back toward the valley, I noticed cottonwoods, sycamore, and walnut in clumps partway up the hillside.

"Strange," I mused aloud. "I'd expect big trees in the valley bottom along a flowing stream, but not up here."

"Oh," said Sarah, "There's a line of springs on the hill, all in a row at the same level."

Not far from the old mine, hidden by trees, we found a reef of quartz as high as a man extending 100 paces from where we stood. It was marbled wonderfully and stained deep-brown with hematite.

"Sarah, there's gold here and silver, too."

"We'll stake a claim! And be rich!" she roared.

"No, we won't," I replied. "We've got to keep it secret."

She looked puzzled.

"The nearest claims office," I explained, "is 300 miles away in Mesilla. There's no law here except us. If we file, we'll have a gold rush and claim jumpers. They'll find out. Someone at the claims office will only tell one 'friend,' and everyone will know. Did you hear what happened at Gila City with Jacob Snively and that awful crew? Soon there were 1,000 men with claims along the river. And they could all come here!"

She looked at me thoughtfully. "I've made good money on such booms by providing food, lodging, and other necessities."

"Yes," I replied, "but you came with the boom and fed it. This time you own the gold. Let's keep it."

Sarah Bowman, the Great Western, had a fine head for business. She nodded understanding and then asked, "How?"

"I've been thinking. Baldy Ewell might be willing to refine our ore along with his own. It'll make his mine look richer, and I trust him. We can hire a few Mexicans, perhaps relatives of your women, giving them and your young ladies small shares to keep our secret. We can dig the Spanish way, rat-hole, or as the German engineers call it, *El sistema del rato,* the rational system. We'll follow the seam, breaking the quartz with heat, water, and iron bars. That way we don't have to buy blasting powder and alert Tucson that something is going on. The result will be a maze of small tunnels.

"Let's see if there's an *arrastra* we can use," I finished. She looked at me quizzically. "A circular rock floor for turning quartz to powder."

"Oh, I know where that is," she smiled and took me to it.

The Spaniards had attached a tiller to a central post and suspended a heavy stone from it. The tiller dragged the heavy stone along the stones of the floor of the *arrastra*. Out beyond the crushing floor, a burro was harnessed to the tiller and induced to walk in circles. In this way, the ore was ground to powder. It could be further refined if you had enough water and equipment by floating off the quartz and stone leaving metallic salts. Gold and silver form amalgam with mercury. Heat the amalgam in a still and what is left behind is sponge gold. The mercury evaporates out of the amalgam leaving behind holes like Swiss cheese or sponge. The mercury is captured for reuse, but don't inhale it or you turn mad as a hatter.

Exploration had used up most of the day. It was too late to start for the rancho when we returned. Besides, before dinner and after, Guadalupe, the girl I'd tried to rescue, insisted on showing me something in her room. Dinner was excellent, too. Sarah's cooking was unsurpassed anywhere. Lighting my nose-warmer I planned to relax enjoying *bacca* and the brandy Sarah had brought. 'Lupe bustled off to find something or other she thought might increase my comfort and pleasure. Increasing my comfort and pleasure would have been difficult as near as I was to ecstasy. I was content and about to be rich. Then a fly intruded into my soup.

Juan Largo leaned over to me and whispered, "Did you make promises to Guadalupe?"

"What?" I asked still in merry spirits.

"Did you make plans for the future with her?"

"No, of course not," I insisted.

"She's telling the other girls that you're going to marry her," said Juan with a grin.

"Gather up your gear! We ride at dawn," I stammered.

I'd soon be a man of substance and consequence. I'd stake a claim to 160 acres, a half mile square of land, containing the house and buildings and a good spring, marking out the corners and drawing a rough map. The government would let a man squat and claim open lands for himself. He had to make improvements, and there couldn't be prior claims, Mexican and Spanish land grants took precedence. The Indians had to have yielded up the land by treaty; they had rights of use only until white people arrived. Juan could claim another 160 acres, and I could buy it from him. Perhaps we could get some friends to do the same. It wasn't really big enough for a ranch. I figured the land might support forty cows and calves per section in the open valley. Initially, we'd own a half section, half of a square mile, 320 acres. That wasn't enough for much of a ranch, but there was plenty of open range around.

We'd brand the cattle in case they mixed with other herds, and there were always fights over who had rights to the grazing. It meant being tough and standing up, usually with a gun, for your rights. Honest ranchers were good about understanding the limits of their grazing rights and that a calf got the brand of its mother. But there were plenty who weren't honest. And there were reivers, what American called rustlers or cattle thieves.

I had a mine as well. That could make a man wealthy. This Arizona was working out well for me, just so long as piskie maidens didn't haunt it and other *buckaboos*. Apache raiders and Mexican bandits were quite enough, thank you.

Mexico was in turmoil and had been since the revolution that ended in 1821. They'd never resolved what they wanted to be. The wealthy *creolos*, Spanish born and descended, wanted a European monarchy and invited European monarchs to intervene. A mixed-blood middle class was strongly Freemason and wanted an American style republic. Poor *Indios*, the most numerous, wanted a socialist country like was being dreamed about by mobs and students in France and Germany. Santa Anna did away with the constitution and imposed rule by the central states. President for Life Santa Anna disenfranchised the border states, Sonora, Texas, California, and New Mexico. There were rebellions. Strapped for funds, Mexico was unable to pay her debts or enforce her rule in the outer provinces. Inability to pay debts and inability to provide services led to rebellions and turmoil, to threats of foreign intervention, and to banditry.

But I'd do all right. I was on my way to being a man of substance, a land owner, a mine owner, wealthy.

Chapter 12 - Apache Trouble

Guadalupe was a nice girl and a good friend, but not the one of whom I'd dreamt. I wanted a wife, someday, but not right now. I wanted a cultured and beautiful woman. Guadalupe was pretty, and she could cook, but she lacked refinement. She came from a *pueblo* where donkeys roamed the street, and people, nice people, thought a tortilla was a spoon. She wore a dress cut so low that it exposed most of her breast, and that wasn't as a result of her profession. That's how all the girls dressed in her village. Western protected her girls. They were nice girls in the business only long enough to raise money for a dowry and maybe to meet someone they liked. I didn't despise her profession. It's what she needed to do to make her way.

She could have married at 14 to some poor man who owned a plot of land that could be covered with a blanket. On it they'd have raised corn, chickens, and children and slowly starved to death. Perhaps she'd have caught the eye of some old man, a widower, who would take her in to raise his children. Some *hidalgo* might have wanted her, but he'd never have married her. She wouldn't have been refined enough for his society. Was I rejecting her for the same reason? I didn't think so.

There was a cultural gulf between us. She was Catholic and Saint Peran rejected my every request even though I was a good Cornishman. Sure, I was Methodist, but that shouldn't matter to a saint. I wasn't a saint, so I could reject Guadalupe for being Catholic. There were differences that both she and I would find irritating in time. There were expectations that would go unfulfilled on both sides, and she would do things that I would think of as disloyalty and even treason. Why, if I were Good King Henry the VIII, I'd soon want to have her head chopped off. So, if you think about it, I was doing her a favor by not marrying her.

Thoughts of hair the color of red gold came unbidden to mind. I saw a fairy princess floating before the wind, lithe of limb, slender and fine, her body the color of milk and just as smooth, nature's child running naked through a pool. I shook my head. Perhaps I rejected 'Lupe because I was *piskie-led.*

Months passed, and life was good. Juan and I settled into our tasks. I gathered more calves and took them out to graze near the headwaters of the Santa Cruz and in the hill country west of the Huachucas. There was good grazing there and water, but dense brush made it difficult to keep track of the herd, and I still had to worry about a feral bull claiming my cattle. Wild bull range was close at hand. In another year or so, I'd have raised a promising bull of my own and turn the other males into steers so they'd grow large and fat and be gentle. My bull would be biddable but fierce, able to protect the herd from predators and keep them together and always moving to good grass. He'd reduce my workload. I'd worry less, but there were other dangers.

Musing on the future, I arrived near the crest of a hill. The herd should be grazing just below.

I stopped short of the crown so only my head was above the hill and gazed into the valley checking for cows and trouble. Stopping and checking the next valley before skylining oneself on the ridge was how one kept alive. The valley floor was grassy with a small stream. My cows were further up the valley than I expected, but they seemed safe.

The hillsides were heavily wooded with oak and manzanita. I rode on.

A young man in Tubac, a mining engineer, fresh from back East, gave me a start stepping out of a doorway in the dusk. He stepped out without a care or a look. Without thinking about it, I checked above for scorpions and centipedes and checked below the sill for rattlers. I sniff the air for javelina and big cat. I stop to see if a black widow spider has made its web across the doorway. Only then do I step through. Smelling, tasting and seeing all these things and even feeling them on your skin is an unconscious act, and the young man made me aware of it. The same applies to riding in Apache country. If you want to stay alive, you check before showing yourself. You look for what should and shouldn't be there and listen for sounds the same way; you smell the air.

I rode into the valley to find that the brush had concealed them, a party of Indians, four of them. And they were butchering one of my calves. They hadn't started a fire yet, or I'd have smelled smoke. They looked at me and stopped moving. I sat my saddle looking right back at them and then calmly packed my pipe, taking my time about it. They were young, well-made men, athletic, and wearing moccasins that came to their knees with that cactus-shaped turned up toe of rawhide. They wore broad cotton loin clothes and loose, colorful cotton shirts, their long black hair bound back away from their eyes by a headband. Two of them had revolvers tucked into their waistbands. Bows and rifles lay on the grass. Four ponies with bridles of plaited horse-hair and rawhide, without saddles, were tied beyond them.

Finished packing, I lit my pipe, puffed, rode to them, and handed the pipe to the nearest one. I motioned that I was headed to the cows and would be back. Then rode over, cut out a calf, and returned with it. I tried Spanish, telling them the calf was for them to take with them. They seemed to understand.

I dismounted and dropped the reins. I trained my horse to be 'ground-tied.' The pipe went around the group and returned to me. Taking it, I took out my bacca pouch and handed it to the one closest brave, telling him to keep it and passed the pipe back around the group. They resumed butchering and gathered wood for a fire. As the meat cooked, I offered them my store of salt.

"You got gunpowder?" one who seemed to be their leader asked in Spanish.

I dug out my powder flask from my 'possibles bag.' "Give you half," I offered.

"*Todo*!" demanded the Apache. "All of it."

"I've given you all of my salt and tobacco," I said hoping to sound both reasonable and more relaxed than I felt. I casually slipped the loop from the hammer of my right-side pistol hoping my move was unobserved. "And you've got two of my calves. Half the powder? I need some, too. What've you got to trade?"

The question caught him off-guard. He had to think about what I meant, and thinking took him past his demand for all the powder.

"Calves ours. Eat grass, drink water on Apache land," he insisted as the others nodded at his wisdom.

"I got the calves away from the big bulls," I countered. "Otherwise, we wouldn't be cooking this one." I could tell that the whole idea of ranching and tending cows had hit home. I walked a narrow path not wanting to suggest they were unable to hunt cows for themselves. "But, you're welcome to some of them," I continued quickly.

The Apache were a canny people. They didn't want to run us off the land. They wanted to continue the arrangement they had with the Pima and Mexican farmers, managing their raids so they didn't take too much and leaving enough for folks to live on. It was how they harvested. They were also great traders bringing goods much needed in the villages from far away. As long as I let them have some, they'd let me do the work of raising cattle, and they'd be the *lairds* of the land. They could play *lairds* if they liked, but I was interested in more than poverty under an Apache *cappen*. I needed to make myself useful.

"What you got to trade?" I inquired again. "I can get cotton, gunpowder, Mexican *aguardiente*, American whiskey, lead, caps, tobacco, and salt. What you got?"

"You get now!" the leader ordered.

"Not now," I replied. "Next time you visit. But you've got to have something to trade." It may sound awful to some ears, but I'd give them small amounts of powder and caps, enough to hunt, not start a war. They were dangerous when drunk, but they'd be sober before they reached a settlement, so most of the danger was to me. I could supply things they had trouble getting. I prayed he wouldn't be bringing me things raided from Mexicans or worse Americans. "I'll have to buy it and bring it here from far away."

He nodded, seeming to understand. He said, "Baskets, tanned buckskin, turkey, slaves . . ."

"No slaves," I cut in. Buying back captives would bankrupt me. Most poor Mexican families wouldn't be able to reimburse me my expenses, and the Apache didn't usually take the wealthy. Ricos protected themselves quite well. I didn't want to encourage raiding.

The meat was cooking and smelled good. Calf is tender. It was time to lay in some *belly-tember.* It looked as though I had another enterprise going and stood to lose fewer cattle. Pleased with *meself*, I was.

Swinging himself up onto his pony's bare back with the grace of an elf; the leader turned and said, "In two moons, we will return to trade." They led away the second calf. I hoped they'd make it past the bulls.

The next morning arrived in *hag* that lingered misty along the *wogmire* and bottoms. Out gathering mavericks toward the Babocomari stream, I let my horse take his own head to find a good pool from which to drink. Nearing the water, I caught sight of the flame-haired *piskie* maiden. *Merrymaids,* my mother taught me, lack legs having only fishtails and thus could not run. She fled and disappeared in mist and brush tangle, reappearing moments later, red hair streaming, as she flew above the brush with hawk speed departing from me.

No, I told myself; it cannot be a real girl. She was too beautiful. "She's only some *fancical* maid," I said aloud. "I will not be *piskie led.*"

I'd seen them in the West Country, Cornwall, the *piskie led;* men who'd chased shadows into forest, fen, and moor, losing themselves. When they returned, if at all, which was seldom enough, they were dazed and confused, never the same again. And they yearned for their *fancical* maidens, saddened the rest of their days at what they had lost.

Real girls don't fly or float above the brush as I'd seen. Her head and shoulders horse-height above the ground rushed away from me through mist and brush and disappeared. Unable to help myself, I tried to follow. Her tiny prints soon faded, and there was nothing else but some fresh tracks of an unshod horse. The mustangs favored this pool. Perhaps she was a fairy horse-minder.

I didn't mention the fairie lass to Juan Largo or Western. They'd have thought me daft. I didn't think they knew much about the fairy folk. In the West Country, we've long studied on them. Morgan the Fay, that means fairy, had lived here bedeviling King Arthur. I'd learned all about his magical court as a boy. And why not? He was born at Tintagel Castle right there in Cornwall. Hadn't Tristan and Isolde been led down fairy paths to betray our own King Mark? Of course, I was cautious of the *piskies*. What rational man wasn't?

At the end of the season, we had 31 calves, now grown to yearlings and 20 cows that had wandered in as well. Fifteen of these were carrying, so our herd would grow the next year.

"It's time, Juan. We must brand them as they wander loose, and we do not want others mistaking them for feral. I've had the blacksmith make me a branding iron. 'Tis an SN slanted for Sin Nombre."

Juan nodded. "I would have preferred a flower or something from nature, the symbol of a mountain or bull. Something strong to protect our cattle."

"Ah, but, Juan, see how the S looks like a lightning bolt descending from a black cloud, the N."

Juan accepted the 'cloud-lightning' brand as a good omen and sharpened his knife.

"See the male calf a little larger than the others? He shall be our bull."

We lit a fire and set to work. I'd rope a calf by the hind legs, throw him, and wait while Juan brought the heated iron. He burned our brand into the rear flank to the stink of burning hair and hide and loose bowels. Then Juan climbed underneath, quickly slashed their testicles, and bit them free with his teeth, finally spitting the *cajones* in a jar.

"Fine eating." He grinned with blood ringing his mouth. He poached some the next morning in chili with eggs. "*Huevos con huevos*," said he.

We finished with the cows and left our young bull intact except for the brand.

I looked toward the heavens. It was late spring, and the grass was dry. I hoped it would rain soon. Blessed, I thought myself, for I saw great clouds rising taller than mountains. In the dry air, they began to crackle with lights within. There would be no rain, yet, but soon.

The wind rose in the southwest. A bolt of lightning struck the ground a mile away. Soon there was smoke, the thick white smoke of burning grass. It choked the lungs and burned the eyes, spreading wide across the valley floor and heading toward us driven by the wind.

"Mount and ride, Don Hombre!"

We rode and our herd preceded us. Soon deer and pronghorns, mountain lions, coyotes, and turkeys mixed in with our herd. Everything was leaving except for the smaller animals with homes underground. I looked behind. The maelstrom was approaching fast with red flames licking higher and higher amid the white smoke.

"Follow the animals," yelled Juan.

"But they're running two points north of the wind. We'll lose time!"

"They know. They go away from the fire, out of its path."

We passed a herd of animals, including some of ours, sheltering in a wash bottom.

"Juan, we've got to get them moving again!"

"No, Don Hombre, they will be safe. The trees and grass down here have good water and will not burn."

We came to the Babocomari and splashed into its stream. "We will be safe here," said Juan Largo.

The fire jumped the stream east of us, but never burned down in the bottoms.

"Cursed fire!" I spat. "We might have lost the whole herd."

"No." Juan shook his head. "The fire is good. The grass will come back. The small mesquites and other bushes that stop the grass from growing have burned. You will see. Our herd is safe, and our range will be better."

The next day, the rains started, and it rained almost every day for a few hours in the coming weeks. The grass came up fine and strong. Our herd returned, and two new cows had joined. Life was good.

I drew maps of our land claims and marked their boundaries. Soon, I'd file these with Poston in Tubac, there being no other land office or government official. I'd make copies for myself to send to Mesilla. The government in Mesilla would want me to appear in person to sign documents and claims. The little Mexican pueblo on the Rio Grande was a long way off, over 300 miles, and could wait. My maps were approximate with there being no surveyed point to tie into; however, I showed reference of distances to Sonoita Creek, the border, Tubac, and the San Pedro River. The land was otherwise unknown and unmapped.

Chapter 13 - Lost Gold

Juan Largo was yarning just at *kindle teening* as we gathered in our supper. "It is said the Jesuits called it *Bella*."

"Called what *Bella*?" I asked.

"Don Hombre," he responded, "your mine, of course. The Franciscans, who came after, who were still here when I was called Juanito, called it the Old Guevari and said it was in the San Cayetano Mountains."

"My mine is not in the San Cayetanos," I said flatly.

"No, it is not," continued Juan, "but it is near. I think the Franciscans did not know. This is why they could not find it, though I know they looked."

I gazed at him thoughtfully. "So, perhaps the mine has an old name. We knew someone had worked it by the rat hole method the Spanish monks employed. Does this help us or mean the monks will arrive to try and claim our *oro*?"

He chuckled. "I think not. They are back in Spain. The Franciscans used to make fun of the Jesuits. They said that those who thought themselves so educated had thrown away the best metal."

"There were many mines in this country," I said. "Why do you think this is the *Bella*, the beautiful?"

Juan pondered a moment, perhaps reconsidering the train of thought that had brought him to this point. "The direction is right, and it is only a little too far. It was the one the Franciscans never found and the one they said the Jesuits treasured most. Because it is a good mine in a beautiful valley. Because of whispers among my people."

"Whispers? What whispers?" I asked, but he went silent, grew reticent. We were friends but the tall, thin, lame old Apache Manso, whose people dwelt among the Wac, the Pima of San Xavier del Bac, would not easily surrender his people's secrets, their whisperings. I had pressed too hard.

We ate our dinner companionably. Laughed and joked and planned.

"Why do you call me Don Hombre?" I asked.

"It is your name, no? Hombre? Or as you say sometimes, Bray."

"Yes," I replied. "But why have you promoted me to don?"

"This," Juan said, "is how we name our elders and men of substance."

"I'm not old!"

"Ah," said Juan, "but you are a man of substance."

"Me? A man of substance? You are joking."

"No," Juan replied. "You have become a *hacendado* with his own *rancho* and the owner of a mine. Soon you will be a trader, too. A man of substance."

"I barely have enough cows to qualify as a *reiver*."

He looked at me quizzically. Although he was picking up Cornish, he didn't understand *reiver*, as yet, our word for a cow thief, a rustler.

"A rustler," I corrected myself, and he nodded. "Besides, I haven't traded with the Apache yet, and I've no license for it." The government licensed all Indian traders and punished those who operated without their approval. The fees and bribes were a source of income for influential Congressmen, and the traders didn't object because narrowing the competition kept profits up more than enough to cover the expense. The government liked to pretend that the license kept the unscrupulous from cheating the Indians and kept the traders from selling guns and liquor to the noble savages. If you believe this hokum, I've got a wee bit of land I'd like to sell you in Cornwall a mite southwest of the Lizard and try not to wet your feet while you're standing on it.

"The Apache will be here tomorrow to trade," said Juan Largo without explanation.

His secret whisperings and strange, seemingly arcane, knowledge of events to come put me on edge and had pondering magic and the wee folk. But I also loaded my two rifles, the shotgun, and all of the pistols making sure they were primed and ready, as did Juan with his weapons. The Apache would trade right well and sharply getting the edge on you in every deal if you weren't careful. But if you looked weak or seemed unlikely to be a future trading partner, they had less expensive ways of getting what they wanted, at least, less expensive for them.

Talk of lost mines and missing gold set my headpiece to thinking on red gold, rich as an orange flame shimmering in sunlight. With my belly well *tembered*, I turned in for the night only to be blessed with troubling dreams of lost gold, which floated like a mane horse-height above the brush. It belonged to a red-haired *piskie* maiden, a *fancical* lass, with a mane the color of orange sunlight. In my dreams, I shadowed her through *hagmire* and desert, but I was never able to catch up, never able to touch her or hold her. Oh, how I wanted to. She was magical, beautiful, and delicate as a flower, and I yearned, nay, burned, for her. I hunted for her and found her hidden under an ancient mesquite a pile of platinum. Looking up, I caught a glimpse of her at the ridge and abandoned this wealth to continue my quest. Again and again, the red-haired lass turned to mere gold or simple platinum, but I rejected them.

I woke in a cold sweat. I had rejected gold! And platinum! And I had done it to chase a *fancical* maiden! Why platinum? Dreaming of platinum, a metal only newly known to men, troubled me almost as much as the thought of being *piskie-led.*

We made our breakfast. Juan was learning to enjoy tea or, at least, to enjoy the mound of sugar he added to it. We set rifles where the muzzles could be seen from outside at each of the upper-floor windows to appear that there were more than just the two of us, but I doubted the Apache would be fooled. They were canny creatures. We checked our weapons yet again, and I crawled down the ladder to the stable and tack room below.

As Juan handed me down my shotgun, he said, "They are near. They circle now looking for weakness and danger."

Having two pistols already strapped on, I set the gun by the door. Juan handed down the trade goods. I would keep them inside the tack room and the Apaches outside, thus controlling any tendency they might have to depart with items before I'd received something in exchange. They were great ones for expecting "gifts."

Six warriors rode up to our gate, and when they'd determined that it was safe, their women and children arrived. I took post at the door to the tack room and wouldn't allow any of them inside though the women and especially the children tried. The women looked things over and told their men what to buy. The trading went well. I'd bring out an item, and they'd make an offer. We haggled a bit, and I'd let them take the item away while I put my acquisition inside and brought out the next item. They wanted flour, pots and pans, knifes, mirrors, cloth, percussion caps, whiskey, and black powder.

The sutler, Elias Brevoort, at Fort Buchanan from whom I bought supplies, might wonder what I was doing with all this stuff, but he held his peace, I think. Perhaps he told Captain Ewell, but telling my old captain would do him little good. We were a long way from enforcement, and Brevoort needed Ewell's friendship. The captain and I, still a soldier then, had been along with Kit Carson when he rode out to save Brevoort's life. Besides, he made money whether I sold it to the Indians or if he did. And he didn't have a license either.

Problems arose when I ran out of goods to trade.

"I want gun!" said the chief.

"I haven't any to trade," I replied calmly, but not feeling calm at all.

"You got many!" he said pointing aloft to the windows. "I trade. You get more."

I nodded. "I'll try to get more, then trade. Guns aren't easy to get." They really weren't, and Ewell and our Sonoita Creek neighbors would notice my buying them. People have a tendency to be mule headed. I guess they have to believe in the superiority of their arms, or they wouldn't come out here surrounded by Apaches. They would think me a traitor for supplying them to Indians. The truth was that the Indians wanted them for hunting. Arrows were better for warfare.

Except for the best rifles, like my Hawken's, the range was under 100 yards. And if you loaded them the way the Apache did, it was even less. They would cut a piece of lead from a plug and chew it into shape. They didn't get them very round, just small enough to fit the barrel. To shoot accurately, you needed to set a completely round ball in a greased patch and ram it home engaging the rifling, the grooves in the barrel, so the ball would spin. The bow and arrow, especially as the Apache handled them, had a range equal to the rifle. But a .50 caliber ball would put a deer into instant shock and drop it in its tracks. An arrow would cause the deer to bleed, and they'd have to follow it until it bled to death. Allowing men to bleed to death in a fight was an advantage. Their companions would have to care for them and drag them along if they wanted to move to a new position. Trading rifles to Apaches would do no one any harm, just like dealing whiskey to them, but it would give me a very bad reputation.

"Maybe next time," I said with finality. "I'll see if I can get any."

The chief looked at the windows again uncertain, I hoped, about how many men he faced. He nodded, turned, and mounted his pony in one smooth motion. His people followed without question.

We shut up the house and stayed inside through the day, making and mending, as the sailormen say. The Apache might be lurking in ambush nearby.

Chapter 14 - Fool's Gold

Fairy maidens with hair red like gold continued to trouble my dreams for days after the encounter.

Finally, Juan could take it no more. "Don Hombre, you are troubled by the spirits. You must go in quest of a vision or surely you will die."

"Ah, but 'tis a vision I am trying to avoid. I have no wish to be *piskie-led*."

The old man looked at me from deep set eyes under gathered brows. "The spirits lead where they will and torture those who will not follow. Great Power seeks you out and will destroy you if you do not abide with it.

"I will say no more." He crossed his arms and stood looking at me in silence.

When I could stand his steady gaze no more, I said, "I've been meaning to visit Brunckow and ask the mining engineer some questions."

I knew even in Juan didn't know my true purpose that I intended to ride down along the Babocomari and follow in the direction the *piskie* maiden had gone. I assured myself that I'd be safe if I followed the stream almost to the San Pedro and then turned off toward Brunckow's mountain. Even if the fairy had gone that way, I wouldn't be following her, and she wouldn't be leading me. I just happened to be heading in the same direction. I was safe, I assured myself.

The river-bottoms were pleasant and full of beaver ponds and cottonwood and here and about stands of walnut. Only the tallest mountains peeked over the tops of the bench, which stood 100 feet high and half a mile apart. Great arroyos penetrate its wall at intervals; otherwise, the desert above hid this green land of flowing water. There were fish and *wee* lobsters in the pools. The fish of a type we called salmon trout were 18 inches long. It was a land the *wee* folk would love; they would be drawn to it as I was.

I'd gone a morning's ride when I heard noise ahead. My first thought was that I hoped it was the *fancical* maiden. I soon was disabused of my wish for the fairie maid when hurrying my horse along I overtook a wagon laden with supplies driven by two boys I'd met over on Sonoita Creek. Joey and Charlie Ake, soon to be teenagers, lived near Fort Buchanan on their father's farm. They were dressed in worn hand-me-downs and wore knee-high moccasins. Boys in this country did not go barefoot. Unprotected feet would come to the attention of rattlers, scorpions, rocks, and thorn and soon reduce them to bloody stumps. Both wore Colt pistols well-oiled, if well-used, and carried rifles. Beside them rode a man strange to me. He was dressed in black frock coat and vest, sombrero, and heavy boots that came to his knees. He had strapped a belt carrying a knife and a pistol over his coat.

The boys were polite. Joey handled introductions. "Mr. St. Gnomebray, this here's Mr. W.M. Williams, super, uh, super-something of the St. Louis Mining Company, which is a fancy way of saying he works for Mr. Brunckow's mine."

"That's superintendent, Joey," said Williams.

"Sure," the boy acknowledged.

"Bray," I said extending my hand. He had a strong grip. "I'm headed to Brunckow's mine."

"Williams or just Bill," he responded.

I was relieved. Surely, the *piskies* wouldn't bother me in such a group. Still I yearned to continue my search for the maiden, certain she would not appear in such company.

We rode through the day and into the evening by a route known to Bill and the boys. They delivered produce for their father. Their track went off at odd directions seeking out places where streams had cut a path large enough for the wagon to pass, ascending, and descending through a land cut by myriad deep arroyos, many with bottoms a quarter mile broad. It was a slower trek than a horse might have done alone but much more companionable. Even the boys were a wealth of interesting news for ones so long isolated.

"The Helligans," Charlie snickered as he said it.

"Sound like hellions to him," Joey whispered.

"The Helligans," Charlie continued with all the dignity he could muster, "Jacko and Tallon and their cousins Turk and Hellyar have been raising all kinds of trouble. Shot men in Tucson and Tubac and at Amado. It's rumored they hold up lone travelers at night."

His brother cut in. "They're very rude to young women. Why just last week on Sonoita Creek, Turk slapped Alice Ann on the bum, and when she squealed, Tallon laughed at her. If Captain Ewell hadn't been riding by just then, I think they would have ravished her further."

"Who's Alice Ann?" I asked.

The elder brother sighed obviously smitten, so Charlie spoke for him, "Alice Ann Crumpton. She's the daughter of our neighbors, the Crumptons. Tall and willowy with long, red hair. Too old for Joey, but he's in love with her anyway. He moons around dreaming of her and sighs and can't speak when she's near."

Joey kicked his brother's shin. "A goddess with peaches and cream complexion who rides bareback as well as any boy and handles a rifle like a man."

Bill, the superintendent, had his hand over his mouth, suppressing a laugh, I thought.

"An elfin goddess," sighed Joey.

It was well after dark, and the stars had long been conducting their procession across the heavens when we arrived at Brunckow's adobe. We hadn't stopped for dinner figuring to get something hot at Brunckow's. A broad, sandy-bottomed wash made our going easier. As we went, we caught occasional glimpses of Brunckow's Mountain to our southeast, a peculiar dark hole in the stars shaped like a volcano.

Bill spoke of Brunckow's Mountain along the way. "That shape, says Brunckow, is lucky for prospectors. There's always minerals near hills like that."

On our left was a high, conical peak we knew to be near the San Pedro. We arrived at the shallow river where it bent briefly east from its northerly course and followed its bottom until we came to a large arroyo entering from the east. We continued up its course another mile. The arroyo bent around a cliff of stone, and there above us silhouetted against the sky was a large adobe building.

"That's strange," said Bill. "I thought they'd have kept the fire going."

Beyond the cliff, we were able to leave the wash and drive the wagon up to the adobe that Bill called Brunckow's cabin. As we approached, I caught a whiff of something evil. Dismounting, Bill called out to his friends within and got no response. He called again and, now clearly concerned, hurried into the building. Emerging in seconds, Bill heaved his breakfast by the door.

I approached and entered, trying not to breathe. Striking one of my two Lucifers, I saw that two men lay on the floor. Before the match burned my fingers, I knew that they had been battered, probably with sledgehammer and pickaxe.

Backing out the door, I said, “Nothing we can do for them. Let’s move back, upwind, maybe to your spring and camp there.” Bill nodded weakly. “I count two,” I continued.

“Where are the others?” he gasped.

“In the morning light will be soon enough.”

Fearing we might again lose the contents of our stomachs, we foreswore breakfast and went to our grizzly task. Bill identified the two bodies as Jack Moss and Jim Peterson. While he pulled them near, I dug a shallow grave and gathered stones to place on top to keep out the prairie wolves. The boys helped with the gathering while trying not to look at the bodies.

Bill growled, “They were beaten to death with their own tools, and every bit of equipment and supplies has been taken. There’s nary a sign of Bontrager and Brunckow or of the Mexicans. Considering what was taken, I’m sure the Sonorans must be the murderers. Things too trivial for a white man to pause over are gone.”

“Where’s the mine?” I asked. “They might have sheltered there.”

“I’ll show you.”

The mine was across the wash about a quarter mile away. Lighting a candle, we descended by ladders into the depths.

Bill yelped in horror. "There's poor Brunckow and the only tool left, a star drill driven through his gut."

"Miserable, slow way to die."

We hauled him out and buried him nearby. Of Bontrager and the Mexicans, there was still no sign.

"We only just hired him," said Bill, "to be our cook. There were eight Mexican peons, too. It's clear to me that Bontrager organized them. I think he watched Brunckow and me hiding our store of gold. I left for Fort Buchanan on Monday."

"Looks to me," I said, "like they've been dead since Tuesday. Today's Friday, so it'll be midday Saturday before we get these boys home. We better get started."

We followed the wash back to the river, this time in daylight and minding the tracks.

"See," said Bill. "I told you. Those tracks show men and our mules headed south along the San Pedro."

I looked and rode ahead 100 paces, scanning the soft, damp sand of the wash bottom, and then calling back, "But there are other tracks. Four or five shod horses headed west toward Sonoita Creek."

Chapter 15 - Sonoita Creek

The chickens scattered as I approached the house. Climbing the ladder from the tack room, I stuck my head into our house where Juan Largo was preparing breakfast.

"*Benvenidos*, Don Hombre," he said. "Breakfast will be ready soon. Tell me of your travels."

The chickens had been a good idea. Eggs and the occasional fowl enlivened our diet. Letting Juan cook breakfast was another matter. Eggs poached in chili with tortillas are hard on the gut of a man raised on bland English cooking. What wouldn't I give for a stary-gazy pie, herrings baked in an egg pie with their heads sticking out to gaze at the stars?

As I waited breakfast, I told him of the murders, the missing Bontrager and Mexicans, and how I had left the others on the trail to attempt to follow the tracks I had found. The summer rains left the ground soft and the imprints deep.

As Juan handed me a plate, I said, "I lost them along Cienega Creek well north of Fort Buchanan."

He nodded. "Headed for Tucson, you think." It wasn't a question, but I nodded anyway. "I do not think Mexicans murdered Brunckow and stole his tools, nor do you."

Juan served himself and tucked in to breakfast with gusto. "We must visit your mine soon. There is something I must show you." He would say only that the Franciscan friars thought it proof that the Jesuit brothers were dumb.

Days later, our first stop was at the sutler's store, Fort Buchanan. The sutler's built his store off to one side apart from the military encampment. It stood at the base of hill across a meadow from the rest of the camp. The post cemetery was on top of the hill. The sutler's store, the post trader, was usually away from the main fort. He sold things the men needed including alcohol. I needed to take supplies to Great Western and hoped some items I'd ordered might have come in.

The buildings of the fort were scattered about like a Mexican village in a very practical, though unmilitary, manner. Most were jacals, stakes driven into the ground side by side and covered with adobe. Located on a hillside above the conjunction of small canyons and sitting beside Sonoita Creek, the place had a closed in feeling. The trader, a civilian, elected by the men or appointed by the post commander, was licensed to sell them the supplies the military did not issue: whiskey, sewing kits, tinned foods, spices and condiments, playing cards, and things found in a general mercantile.

Elias Brevoort greeted me. "Welcome, friend, or should I say, sergeant? It finally came to me where I seed you before. 'Twas on the Santa Fe Trail. You was ridin' with Capn' Ewell then, and you come with Kit Carson to save my life. You carried a different name then, but I'll respect your privacy."

I managed a smile and took his hand, although I was not happy that he recognized me with the Helligans in the area. Being known was not good news. The more people who knew a secret, no matter how well intentioned, the less time it had to stay secret.

Brevoort was good at anticipating needs. His store was the only one in the Sonoita Valley, and all the miners, stockmen, and farmers, along with the soldiers, came here for what they needed. For soldiers, he stocked buttons, shiny brass ones, needles and thread, sewing kits, shoe polish and pipe clay, quills, ink, and stationary. Many, if not most, could write and wrote home frequently. Men from Germany, Ireland, and France were in the ranks, of course, but many were farm boys out looking for adventure and a way west to the promise of the frontier. There were also bummers and ner' do wells, of course, and drunkards, but many of these tended to desert at first chance, leaving behind a legacy in the commander's memory, for these were the ones he got to know most intimately.

There was a story then current about Captain Ewell. The *cappen*, the story said, had had a man so inept in drill that he told him to get off of the fort and not come back. The man stole Ewell's best horse and headed south. Naturally, Ewell pursued him into Sonora and brought him and, more importantly, the horse back. There was a rumor that while in Sonora the boy married an alcalde's daughter. Brevoort and I laughed over the boy's choice of horseflesh and his good fortune.

Brevoort sold liquor, of course. He imported brandy, wine, and champagne for the soldiers and his other clientele but getting it was difficult. Supplies either came by ship to Guaymas and by mule train up through Sonora or to Fort Yuma and over the desert trail along the Gila. Either way was expensive. Only officers could afford the good bottled liquors, and there were seldom more than six officers at Fort Buchanan. Beer was impossible, too bulky to import, and no one locally was brewing it. Whiskey was the order of the day, but even bottled whiskey was expensive to ship, so Elias bought it by the barrel as pure grain alcohol. When it arrived, he cut it by half with water and added molasses and tobacco for color and taste.

"I put it in bottles, and they think they're drinkin' the good stuff. I use the bottles over and over." He grinned.

For farms, ranches, and mines, he stocked black powder, percussion caps, blasting caps, and fuses. Guns were available, along with salt, pepper, spice, flour from the mill at Silverlake near Tucson, both wheat and corn flours, saleratus, and canned vegetables. He had canned meats as well and sardines in tins that came all the way from France.

Eager to share news, as was a merchant's want, Elias said, "Big doin's at the Boundary Hotel. Bontrager has come in, and they're tryin' him. Paddy Graydon's playin' host."

Finishing my business as quickly as possible without giving offense, I hurried out wanting to see the results of the hearing at the Boundary, knowing as I did so that it was a mistake to go near Paddy. I'd try to be unobtrusive, but Paddy Graydon knew me and knew me well. We were both graduates of Ewell's Company G, 1st Regiment of Dragoons.

The Boundary Hotel offered everything a soldier might want but couldn't find in the mess hall or sutler's store, if you catch my meaning. A rambling single-story adobe structure, it stood on a hill overlooking Sonoita Creek about three miles south of post. As Juan and I approached, we saw many horses tied up outside and not a few wagons, which indicated that the gentry had arrived. There were no fancy carriages in Arizona as yet. Poking my head into the door of the sala, the great room, I glanced about and listened.

Bontrager had indeed returned to the area and been captured. His story was that the Mexicans had murdered the others and forced him to go with them as they fled to Mexico, keeping him as a hostage until they got there. The Mexicans' names and home villages were known. W.M Williams read them off from his ledger book. The mine managers and owners, often one and the same, had gathered. All of the mines employed Mexican workers and any uprising that might become general was a common concern. These community leaders determined to release poor Mr. Bontrager who had been for days in fear for his life from the savage Mexicans. They would also send a letter to the governor of Sonora and some of the influential citizens, requesting that they detain the Mexican workers and send them back for trial. Paddy Graydon was in the crowd, and I endeavored to keep my hat between him and myself.

When the recently freed Bontrager stood, I saw that we had met. I knew him by another name, in another place: Seamus O'Malley of Santa Fe.

Then Paddy was on me, extending his hand to greet me. "Ooomph!" I punched him just below the ribs just hard enough to silence him and taking his arm dragged him outside before he could say more.

"Mr. Graydon, is it? I'm Bray St. Gnomebray," I introduced myself. "Call me Bray."

"Do call me Paddy, me lad," he said rubbing his stomach. "Have we met?" He was quick on the uptake.

"Not in this life," I replied with a wink and then changed the subject. "Do you know this Bontrager?"

"No," replied Paddy. "Except for Williams, nobody seems to know him. Why?"

"I knew him by another name in Santa Fe, Seamus O'Malley."

Paddy nodded. "I've heard the name. He's bad news. What do you plan?"

I thought a moment. "I don't want to give myself away. His friends are looking for me, but I hate to see a murderer go free. I'll have to tell the lairds o' manor."

"Nay, lad," Paddy responded. "What would be the point? They've nary a jail and no authority to hang him. The court is way over in Mesilla. He'd never make it to trial."

I nodded, thinking. "What about the Mexicans accused?"

He chuckled. "Don't give it a thought, me boyo. Do you really think the governor of Sonora will round them up so we can hang them?"

"Good seeing you, Paddy. Not a breath of a word of me name. I'd better get out of here before O'Malley recognizes me." Having told Paddy not to reveal my secret, Juan and I mounted and rode south toward Casa Blanca to tend to the mine and apply ourselves to more tender matters.

As we rode along the creek, I espied a maiden leading a cow across a meadow. Fair she was with hair like red gold and no *fancical fairie* lass was she, but real. Fairies may steal the cow's milk in the night, but they never tend them in the daylight. Entranced, I wandered from the road and approached the apparition. The closer I came the more beautiful she became. A thin cotton dress that covered her from neck to ankles revealed her slim figure. She sang as she walked a siren song, a mix of honey, cream, and saffron.

She looked up revealing stunning green eyes. “Can I help you, mister?” Her voice was sweet as silver bells ringing.

I wanted her to speak more, I sitting there atop my horse gazing down like a mooncalf. Stunned, my mind chose to speak aloud its hidden thoughts.

“Delicate and fine as a spring flower its petals flaming red reflect light like gold.”

“Mister, are you okay?” she asked. “Too much sun?”

“Green orbs like limpid pools possessed of water fairies drawing me in to my doom. Hair the color of saffron and a scent on her like the same. ‘Tis the scent of home, of Cornish baking.”

“Excuse me?” She blushed. Her fair skin let the blush stream through in all its glory, glowing like the sun. I felt a moth before a flame.

“Don Hombre, we best vamoose!” said Juan. “Her father’s coming with a shotgun.” He grabbed my reins and led me back to the trail.

Chapter 16 - Platino!

Juan tried to rouse me from my dream-state as we rode on toward Casa Blanca. All I could see was that angelic face crowned in red-gold. All I could hear was her voice like tinkling bells.

"Amigo," Juan said, "I think you are *piskie-led*!"

He awakened some deep fear, and I began to sweat, cold, clammy sweat. Still, I did not return to the land of men. I wandered instead into the gardens of the *piskie* maiden, unwilling to return.

Who was I to mooncalf over a slip of a girl? I who had been smuggler captain, dragoon sergeant in the best and toughest company in the army, and who was a trader with Apaches was no man to quail before a maiden. I'd ridden alone for many years through hard company and tough times. I'd killed men when I had to and faced hardship without complaint. Moreover, I knew the ways and wiles of the fairy folk and could not be fooled. How could I be taken like a child with his first puppy? I'd known and loved grown women.

"Don Hombre," Juan called to me, trying to draw me back. "Don Hombre! We must talk of great wealth and ignorant Jesuits."

Wealth got my attention. One ear perked up and listened, the other still alert for the song of silver bells, the song of honey, cream, and saffron that tasted of Cornwall and home.

"Wealth?"

"Wealth!" he affirmed. "Better than gold?"

"What could be better than gold?" I laughed. He had pulled me back. Both ears were listening as we rode to the ranch along the Babocomari Stream, the shortest way from the Sonoita Valley.

Juan nodded but looked at me darkly. "They said it was white, whiter than silver, and did not tarnish black like silver, and it was soft like gold and very valuable."

"Platinum?" I asked.

"*Si, si*, they called it *platino*!" he said. "It sounds like silver, *plata*, no?"

I nodded. "So what of this *platino*? My mine produces gold and some silver."

Juan grew thoughtful. "I believe your mine is the Bella, hidden by the Jesuits when they were forced to leave, keeping their wealth from the Franciscans who never discovered it. The friars were searching in the San Cayetano Mountains too far to the west. There was *platino* in the Bella. That's why she is Bella!"

I looked askance at Juan. "How can our mine be the Bella? It does not produce platino."

Juan looked at me and nodded slowly. "Perhaps you will yet find platino. Or maybe you will find where the Jesuits threw it away."

I coughed, nearly falling off my horse. "What?!?"

"They threw it away," Juan said. "That is why the Franciscans thought them stupid."

If he was right, a fortune was lying on the ground near the mine. But how could Jesuits throw it away, and how would Franciscans have known?

Unbidden, Juan responded. "The Jesuits made a little plate for the altar to serve the communion wafer. They didn't know what the plate was made of. It was soft, white metal; tin they thought. This plate was left at San Xavier del Bac. When the Franciscans came, they saw it and asked questions. One of them recognized the metal, but the people could only tell them it came from Bella, and the Jesuits had thrown most of it away."

I knew that metals occurred in pockets in the mine. Prospectors found sulfides and chlorides in different places, along with the metals that bonded with them. Platinum was possible. It might go unnoticed and be taken for tin or lead or even iron pyrite, which in crystalline form looks like silver, hence the Spanish name platino meaning little silver. Spain drove out the Jesuits out in 1767. Metallurgists first identified platinum in the middle of the 18th century, so it was possible that the Jesuits hadn't recognized it. To them it was still unknown.

"We'll have to search for it," I stammered.

"You are a wise man, Don Hombre," said Juan, pleased that I'd accepted his conclusion. I was sure he had other reasons for arriving at it than those he'd given, little bits of knowledge gathered here and there.

I pondered. Could a mine produce silver, gold, and platinum? Of course, it could, and copper, nickel, iron, lead, and other things. An iron ore called hematite was scattered on the ground near the arrastra. It was shiny, black, and heavy, but of little use to us. We lacked the equipment to refine it further, and it was too heavy to ship easily. Quartz and crystals of numerous ores filled the cracks in the rocks, the veins that we followed. In different seams, different ores predominated. We were set up to refine silver and gold, which were the easiest to process cheaply and the most valuable making it worthwhile to transport them. We ignored and threw away many ores because we had no convenient way to retrieve the metals locked in them. Platinum came from the earth almost pure.

If the miner could break away the quartz, what was left was sand and platinum. With so many ways to retrieve the metal from the sand, why would anyone throw it away?

I spoke aloud to myself, "Why? Why would anyone throw platinum away?"

Juan Largo answered, "Because it is very rare and they did not recognize it."

"We have to be careful, Juan. We might start a rush and be overrun with fools and criminals."

He nodded.

We had news of what was happening at Colorado City near Fort Yuma. There were placers in the sands along the Gila River. Men from the California gold fields flooded in. They knew how to work placers. The river had done the hard work of wearing down mountains and grinding quartz to sand, releasing flakes of gold to settle in the first place where the river slowed and dropped its heaviest sand. There was madness and shootings as men jumped each other's claims. There were jealousies and fights among men angry with sellers of whiskey, tools, women, and games of chance who came to fleece those who found a prime spot. And then, all too fast, the rich dirt that had taken ages to accumulate was gone, and the men, prospectors, miners, gamblers, whore-masters, and claim jumpers were off like a cloud of locusts for some new spot. There wasn't enough water to work the remaining placers. Soon only Sonorans remained, working four to a blanket tossing shovelfuls of dirt to let the mind take away dirt, dust, and sand, leaving the heavy gold. A team could make $5 or even $6 in a day of backbreaking labor.

"Not here," I mumbled, and Juan seemed to understand.

We kept our efforts hidden by processing our ore in the Spanish method with a hidden arrastra, a heavy rock suspended by a pivot arm above a stone floor. A burro dragged the arm, and the rock crushed quartz. We gathered gold and silver from ground-rock with mercury, which forms an amalgam with both, and then heated it in a retort to recover the mercury for reuse, which left the sponge gold and silver behind. Careful not to attract attention, we shipped our metal with the product of Captain Ewell's mine, as though it were his.

Word of platinum might get about. It was unexpected and might draw attention especially if there was as much as Juan thought already lying about on the hillside under some juniper or oak tree.

"We'll tell the Great Western," I said indicating our red-headed Amazon partner, "and then we'll search."

It was days before we again returned to the Casa Blanca and the mine. It wouldn't do to be too anxious and upset routine.

Arriving near the Casa Blanca, how appropriate that name seemed now, for platinum is white. We scouted carefully to see who was about. Maria, the girl standing guard behind the parapet on the roof, waved to us. The girl was calm and friendly and her demeanor was a good sign that all was well. Still and all, the Pellewes, the Helligans, or Dave Bontrager/O'Malley might be near. Juan went in first. Most gringos wouldn't notice him, passing him off as Mexican even though he was an Apache because he didn't dress the part of the mountain warrior.

Juan returned shortly. "Paddy Graydon is here with a man I don't recognize, and they *be elbow crookin'*." This be *kicklish*; Juan was pickin' up me manner 'o speech. I must have been distracted with the fairy maid longer than I'd thought.

We went in together. Paddy was sitting with Palatine Robinson, same as I'd met in Mesilla, and it was clear he recognized me, though Sarah Bowman, the Great Western and madam of this establishment, got to me first and greeted me with a hug that would have slain a lesser man.

As she released me, Palatine spoke, "And is the devil still on the loose in Arizona?" Without waiting a reply, he said pointedly, "I've met another who calls the Dark Lord *Tantarabobus*."

Recalling our past relations, I nodded politely to him and thanked the One *Abew* that our parting had been genial. I'd won his money, but he seemed unaware that I had deliberately evaded his attempt to rob me. He hadn't realized that I knew what a crook he was.

"Care to give me a chance to win my money back," Palatine said pleasantly.

I paused too long recalling. Sensing something amiss, Sarah cut in. "Mr. Robinson was just offering to find ladies for me as well as seeking a concession to deal *monte* at my tables."

"And offering the same to me," said Paddy.

I suspected that if Palatine was dealing in ladies, families would be missing their kidnapped daughters in Mexico. He was a Southerner and a slaver. Monte was a Mexican card game much like our faro. It was a *wifflehead's* game guaranteed to make the house money. I noticed there were no cards on the table. Paddy was probably too smart to play with Palatine Robinson, but you never knew with Paddy. He thought himself pretty smart and might *figger* he could turn the tables on this *gaert pilliock* of a tinhorn gambler. Sarah would want no part of girls who hadn't come to her willingly for her protection.

Both Sarah and Paddy would be looking to be rid of Mr. Robinson without offending him or his friends.

"I've backers," said Palatine meaningfully over-stressing the word, "who can supply both women and monte dealers. They'll be disappointed if you don't accept."

Chapter 17 - Dance with the Devil

"Come to the kitchen," said Sarah, bustling me out of the room. "I've got something to show you."

I waved to Paddy. "See you in a few."

Out of the room, as tall as I with red hair, Sarah looked me in the eye. "What do you know of this Palatine Robinson?"

I gave her query a moment's thought, knowing people respected more an answer that wasn't hasty, and then said, "He cheats at cards, but not well. And he's not above knocking a man on the head to recover his gambling loss. He sells girls into slavery. Worst of all, his comment about another who says *Tantarabobus*, meaning Satan, was pointed. He implies he's backed by the Helligans."

She "ooophfed" like she'd been hit in the stomach. We'd had trouble with them once before. They'd dumped me down the shaft that became our mine and left me for dead.

"Aye *cappen*, *Tantarabobus* is on the loose, and we're in for a *capperause*."

Quick on the uptake, she said, "So, they're after Paddy's business and mine."

"Seems so."

She was silent a long time. "Do you see any way to be rid of them?"

I had to think on that a while. There was no law to back Sarah and Paddy, and, if there had been, the law might still hesitate to become involved because of the nature of Paddy's and Sarah's businesses. Gambling was legal and so was operating a home for young ladies of few means, but the better folk tended to look down their long noses at them.

Finally, I responded. "We could bury Mr. Palatine Robinson in the kitchen garden and butcher his horse, which might otherwise be recognized. That will cause a delay while they try to figure out what's happened to him and designate another emissary. But, sooner or later, you'll have to decide to leave or fight, and you're outnumbered."

She took the warning that she'd be outnumbered as an insult to her abilities and got her back up. "I been outnumbered before down in Mexico, as you'd do well to recall." At Buena Vista, she'd turned the volunteers who ran back into the line to face Santa Anna once more, more scared of her than of the enemy, and then she'd drug away the wounded under fire. They say the dragoons and flying artillery, who moved about the battlefield seeming to be everywhere at once, turned the tide of battle for General Taylor, outnumbered as he was five to one. Those of us who were there know Sarah was the rock, which broke Santa Anna.

"If you partner with this lot in any way," I said, "they'll take more and more until instead of protecting your girls, you'll be taking advantage of them. The games will be so crooked, even Paddy won't like it."

She gave a small smile at that. We both knew Paddy was a rapscallion, but not a villain.

"So there's two of us to face them," she said. "Got any good news?"

I nodded. "As a matter of fact, I do. Juan thinks our mine is the Jesuits' Bella and that they left platinum scattered on the ground."

"Tush!" she hissed, suggesting I was teasing. Platinum was not well known, nor did it occur in abundance, but Sarah was nobody's fool. "Enough of your fairy tales."

Just then Guadalupe and Luz, two of Sarah's raven haired beauties, joined us, grabbing my arms, and pulling close until I could feel the warmth of their bodies.

Guadalupe giggled, "He's mine. I will marry heem. But tonight, *mi hermana*, we can share!"

As delightful as that idea should have sounded, I couldn't rise to the occasion. A *fancical fairie* maiden with red-gold hair filled my heart and mind. I wanted no part of *dolly moppin'* with the love of my life just down the canyon. Bending I kissed one and then the other politely on the forehead but was *taddly-oodly* with thoughts of Alice Ann. I could think only of my fair maiden. The girls snuggled closer and began dragging me toward a more private spot. I was *arry* a priest nor about to shave *me* head and go east and become one, but there is such a thing as wastin' what the *One Abew* hath provided. Perhaps, I pondered, if I thought only of Alice Ann as I caressed these dark beauties. . . Thinking of another woman as I lay with them hardly seemed fair to Luz and Guadalupe. Besides, the latter had announced her intention to wed me.

That was like a bucket of cold water. For the first time ever, I just couldn't, and the girls went away disappointed. It was the beginning of a cruelly disappointing evening.

Back in the *sala*, Juan huddled in the corner with a lass whose tender years were far behind her. A bit over the hill, perhaps, but Juan seemed to have found good grass on the other side, and the pair soon disappeared.

"Cards?" Palatine questioned hopefully.

There was nothing for it, no means of escape, so Sarah and I settled in with Paddy and Robinson who produced a dog-eared deck. It didn't take long to figure out his marks. Paddy and Sarah were onto him as well. Poker takes on whole new horizons when everyone knows what the others are holding, especially when at least one person at the table doesn't know that the others know. Palatine Robinson just wasn't much good at cheating, but it was his deck so we played along.

I packed, lit my nose-warmer, and took a few slow puffs. The sala smelled of tobacco, sweat, cheap perfume, and Sarah's cooking. My mind drifted, not paying as much attention as I ought to the game. I thought of a fairy maid. I didn't know her. I'd only seen her, barely spoken to her.

I could vouch that Sarah and I didn't make a practice of cheating. We just didn't like anyone making sport of us. Paddy didn't make his living cheating, but he wasn't above fleecing a tenderfoot for amusement.

Palatine held a pair of twos, drew two cards, and got no help, but tried to bluff. Holding three kings, I made a small raise, as did Paddy and Sarah. I don't know if they suspected what I was about, or if they simply followed my lead. Palatine continued to bluff and raise. As the pot built to a moderate size, Sarah and then I folded. Palatine made an extravagant raise, suggesting great confidence, and Paddy holding two pair finally folded and let him have the pot. Knowing that we had better cards, Palatine Robinson was now quite pleased with himself and his ability to bluff. He was over-confident and convinced he was about to fleece fools. Poker isn't about the cards; it's about understanding people.

We played him deliberately losing small pots to him and occasionally a larger one to make him happy, while we passed around winning pots between us and slowly whittled him down bit by bit. When he appeared discouraged, we let him bluff his way to an *ansum* pot.

Sometime well after midnight, he was down to trying to get credit for his watch and vest. In Mexico during the war, Sarah, two of her girls, and I had played a game where credit was allowed on clothing. We'd gotten to know each other much better as a result. There was a certain lack of appeal to sending Robinson back to Tucson riding bareback, so we did not allow the vest as proper collateral.

"I have this golden locket with a tintype of my wife," he offered.

I looked at it. "*Ansum*, uh, handsome woman, but I think not. If you can't meet my raise, I guess you're done."

"But, but…" he sputtered, trying to come up with an excuse. I'm sure he did not wish to return to the men he represented freshly shorn. "I can get more money," he said. "I'll give you an IOU."

"Sorry," I replied. "Could be months or years before I see you again."

He looked to Paddy and then Sarah, but found no help. He was done for the night and begged Sarah for a room. No one would want to ride the canyons in the dark.

In the late morning, Sarah fixed him breakfast and sent him on his way.

Paddy watched him go. "That's not the end of it, you know," he said.

Sarah glanced at Paddy. "Almost as effective as burying him in the kitchen garden."

"And *fer* certain that," I said. "It will cause confusion to the enemy. They'll wonder did their emissary fail because he was a fool. They'll ponder sending forth a new one. It buys us time. But not much, I think."

Chapter 18 - Beauty is as Beauty Does

It was a fine, beautiful morning when Robinson rode away. I climbed onto the roof and joined Guadalupe on watch. In those times, before the War Between the States, the Apache were not so murderous as they later became. Lone travelers were apt to disappear, maidens were carried off into bondage, but mostly the Apache wanted livestock and goods at little risk. If one kept careful watch, he was less likely to be robbed. And so, the Casa Blanca, a house of women in the heart of Apache country, survived. They traded with the Indians and gave them meals but kept a loaded gun to hand at all times.

The Mexican lass turned her dark eyes full on me. "*Querido*, you are mine. *Besame mucho*, *mi corazon.* Do not turn from me. Do not hesitate. Is there another? If so," she said pulling a large knife from the folds of her skirt, "I have *un cuchillo grande* to cut out her *corazon, no*?"

"No!" I protested. "There is only you."

"I will cut off her *cabeza*," she continued. The knife was big enough.

I packed *me nose-warmer,* struck a *Lucifer*, and shared the smoke with Guadalupe, who much preferred cigars rolled in corn husk. *Cigaritos* she called them. I exhaled smoke and filled my lungs with warm, fresh air as I turned about enjoying the scenery. The hill country was green with trickling streams and ponds teeming with beaver, not like the sandy deserts and burnt prairies only a few miles distant. Life, for the moment, was good. Down the canyon a flame-haired wonder approached leading two pack animals. I stood entranced, unable to pull away.

Guadalupe tugged my arm. "Eet eez only Alice Anna, *una chiquita* who brings *leche y huevos*, milk and eggs, from her father's *rancho de leche*, milk ranch."

She saw my expression and flew into the sudden rage common to her people.

"This is only a *chiquita*, a little girl!" she protested. "You are mine!"

She raised her rifle and aimed it at Alice Ann. The sound of the hammer being cocked froze my heart.

Before I could react, Guadalupe lowered the rifle and spoke. "No, I like her *mucho*. Maybe I let her have you."

I watched the *piskie* princess approach, enthralled as she tied up her animals, and removed a basket of eggs padded in hay and a sealed jar of milk from the pannier. She disappeared inside. I ran to the ladder, but Guadalupe stopped me, putting a finger to her lips.

"You watch. I go," she said. Handing me the rifle, she slid down the ladder to greet Alice Ann. I was relieved until I recalled Guadalupe was carrying *un cuchillo grande* and had sworn to cut out her rival's heart. Then my heart raced.

I ran to the ladder and started down to the upper story. From far below, I heard girls giggling. At the stairs, I lay down on the floor and stuck my head down to look into the *sala* below.

Sarah's young ladies had Alice Ann surrounded. One brushed her red hair while another applied red lacquer to Alice's fingernails; a third was rouging Alice's lovely dove-white cheeks, and a fourth and fifth approached with a fancy dress and earrings.

Somewhere in the melee Guadalupe could be heard proclaiming, “We must make her look *una novia*, a bride, for our Don Hombre!”

The mention of brides and marriage made me shudder. It was all happening much too fast.

Just then a voice boomed, “Guadalupe! Aren’t you supposed to be on guard?” Sarah entered the room, and Guadalupe bolted for the stairs. On the run, she shoved by me, grabbing her rifle from my hands as she passed.

I picked myself up from the floor and dusted myself off. Too late. Sarah, the Great Western, looking up the stairs after Guadalupe, had detected my presence.

“Bray! Get on down here,” the Great Western ordered.

I descended meekly to my fate. The sea of women parted revealing a freshly spiffed *fairie* queen who needed no enhancements nature had not already provided for her. She was heart-stopping beautiful.

“Bray,” said the Great Western, “I’d like you to meet Alice Ann Crumpton.” Alice curtsied. I almost took her hand to kiss it, but I bowed in my most courtly manner instead. “Alice’s father runs a milk ranch, and she brings us milk and eggs and such.”

“Charmed,” said Alice Ann, but she didn’t know the half of it. Her face told a different story. An old woman, more mature, might have told Sarah that we’d already met and that I was, in her opinion, very strange. That I talked oddly, acted like a mooncalf, and said strange things. But this was a maiden, unblemished and innocent. I doubt she understood the purpose of Sarah’s house. These were just her girlfriends. She was a little afraid of the strange man twice her age.

"The pleasure is mine, Milady," I replied.

Sarah had waved away the fancy dress so Alice remained clad in simple gingham, her hair tied in silk bows, earrings hammered from silver coins dangling from her precious lobes. Sarah's ladies continued to bustle about like a pack of dogs joyful at their master's return. Before long, one of these jubilant creatures, returning from the kitchen, hung a basket from my arm, and the throng of happy sisters pushed Alice Ann and me toward the door.

"To the *ojos*," suggested Maria. I don't know if she meant we should walk to the spring or that I should look Alice Ann in the eye. I tried both, gazing into limpid pools of crystalline green.

The basket contained a picnic of cold chicken, biscuits, white wine, and tidbits, some of them blazingly spicy, from the Casa Blanca. I spread the blanket provided under a cottonwood tree and seated Alice Ann upon it. Pouring wine for both of us, I was surprised that one so young accepted, though it was soon clear that she had no experience of spirits.

The wine gave life to her tongue. I asked about her life and aspirations, saying little about myself, taking joy in listening to the tinkling bells that were her voice and reply. There was *fairie* magic here, and I was *piskie-led,* forgetting myself my troubles, wandering through green hills and forest vales following her voice.

They say smells recall deep memories, and 'tis true. The odor of a fresh opened can of sardines took me back to me mother's Cornwall kitchen and the aroma of a new-baked *stary-gazy pie*, herrings in a circle with their heads sticking out, baked in egg and onion, covered with a warm blanket of dough. But what of sounds? The tinkle of her voice brought to mind strolls through forest glades with the spring a crystal pool that faded into eyes of green as a lost and lonely traveler found safe haven. West Country stories tell of *piskie-led* men disappearing into the forest for years and years and sometimes forever. I was ready to be led by the *fairie* princess.

She prattled like a child, but I hardly noticed. Her voice rang like tinkling bells.

It was late afternoon before Alice Ann and I returned to the Casa Blanca. Wonder of wonders, she had her arms wrapped tight about my arm and her head upon my shoulder. The thought crossed my mind that she thought of me like a father. I dismissed it. I was in love, completely *piskie-led.* Sarah and I accompanied her home, hurrying to get her there before the darkness fell, I, hanging back at the last, so as not to be seen by her father.

As we turned into the gloom to ride back to Casa Blanca, Sarah turned to me and said, "You know we've still got a problem with the Helligans."

She distracted me from another problem. A girl, not a woman, that I was in love with who was much too young. It was nice of Sarah to include me into her business problems, I thought, and then realized that any way you cut it, I had a problem, too. Sarah had wisdom, and she also knew that I left Santa Fe ahead of outlaw retribution and came to Arizona hoping to find my fortune.

Tucson was a snake's den populated by men on the run from the San Francisco Committee of Vigilance or from eastern justice who thought themselves safe so far from the law. The Helligans were organizing its evil to threaten the rest of Arizona, that is to say, Tubac and Sonoita Creek, all the rest there was in the 1850s. There was no way to oppose them. There were no courts, no Federal marshals, and no sheriff. Being part of Doña Ana County, we had no right to elect or appoint any law officers. The government not only didn't provide us any defense, but by leaving us unorganized, denied us the right to defend ourselves. It was no wonder the Helligans thought they could get away with murder and worse. There was no one to oppose them. Of course, they hadn't counted on the independent nature and toughness of Arizona pioneers. Men who face Apaches alone are not easy pushovers. They just have to find a way to organize themselves when the government won't allow it.

My sleep was not troubled, well, not troubled by bad men and business problems. I dreamt of a *fairie* princess with red-gold hair and of our time together under a cottonwood tree. I could feel the warm pressure where she held onto my arm.

Chapter 19 - The Courtship of Miss Alice Ann

Back at Casa Blanca, Sarah and I sat in a corner drinking *aguardiente.* I'd have preferred beer, but the making of it was too difficult for this remote land. We were lucky to get anything better than tequila, cactus whiskey. The room filled up with smoke, talk, and men, some Anglo farmers and ranchers, a few soldiers, and many Mexicans. Sarah's ladies circulated, whispering suggestions in men's ears as they drank, and gambled. Guadalupe dealt *monte* for a table of excited *paisanos*.

"So," said Sarah, "how do we go about finding this *platino*?"

"Do we have time to think about this?" I asked astonished.

Sarah smiled. "It'd be a nice stake for leaving the country."

I looked at her long and hard, uncertain of what she meant. Backing down from a fight was not like her. She was a *pragmatical* creature to be sure, but she didn't like being pushed or threatened and took things on her own terms. I figured she'd organize and fight the Helligans no matter the cost.

"Well," I finally responded, "I suppose the platinum would have come from a single ore-body, so it should be in one place. They brought it up thinking it was something else, silver maybe, and in the light of day saw it wasn't, so they dumped it."

She nodded, "There are a dozen places where their rat holes broke surface. Which one?"

I thought a bit. "Hard to say. We need to check the ore dumps and around the smelters. It must be buried."

Downing the last of her drink, Sarah said, "Tomorrow, when we search, be thinking about solutions to the problem Palatine Robinson has left us."

The next day we set out separately, Juan, Sarah and I, walking parallel courses over the hills, then changing places, and going back over the ground the others had covered. Sketching what we saw, we created a map.

Sarah called out, "Hey, I've found something!" We gathered to her, and she handed me a heavy, shiny black rock with smooth almost melted sides, so silvery black it shone.

I spat on it, rubbed my fingers in the spit, then pulled them away, and showed them to Juan and Sarah. My fingers showed blood red. "Hematite," I said. "Iron ore . . . but that's good. It was thrown away, and the platinum ore might be near."

"*Si*," said Juan, "the Franciscans laughed that the Jesuits had thrown it away. So strange, holy men who are jealous of each other."

We went over that pile of hematite carefully, turning over lumps of ore, digging down and checking around the edge of the pile, but found nothing.

"We'll come back and turn the pile over completely," I offered. "For now, let's try to find other piles like this."

Juan pointed uphill. "There is one there." He showed us on the map, and Sarah indicated another more distant mound of ore.

"Enough for today," I said. "We're losing the light."

Emerging from the kitchen after dinner, I found the *sala* already filling with soldiers, *charros,* and prospectors.

"Come here," called Sarah. "There is someone you should meet."

She sat at a table on the lap of a gray-bearded man in coveralls, nibbling his ear, a tin cup of what I assumed was tequila before him. Skin burned by the sun till it looked like old leather, his age was hard to judge. He was a big man with powerful shoulders and large, calloused hands. A rifle leaned against the wall near to hand, and, while he wore a large knife, he had no sidearm.

"Bray," said Sarah, "I'd like you to meet Abner Crumpton. Abner this is Owen Bray St. Gnomebray." *Hombre sin nombre*, the man with no name; he cocked an eyebrow at that.

"Forgive me," he said extending his hand, "if I don't stand. Wouldn't want to dump Maria on the floor." He chuckled, but his face registered nothing else.

I choked for a second and then responded, "Call me Bray. Pleased to meet you."

"Likewise. Call me Abner. Have a seat."

Sarah's eyes twinkled, but she gave nothing away. "I've known Bray a long time since he was a youngster in the Mexican War. I trust him, and I've partnered with him from time to time."

"Good to know." Abner nodded. Maria stuck a tongue in his ear, and he was distracted for a while returning the favor.

"Abner has a lovely daughter," said Sarah. "She has a handsome figure and dresses herself well and has lovely red hair like mine."

"Aye," said Abner, "and she's of an age to give me fits. Pretty she is and almost an old maid at sixteen. There's few suitable men about, but she won't look at none of them. I don't know what to do. My neighbor Ake's lads are all too young, and I won't have her with an enlisted soldier. Perhaps an officer, but she pays them no mind."

Under the table, Sarah kicked me in the shin. Maria threw a liplock on Abner that nearly took them both out of the chair. His hand moved to cup a buttock and then a breast.

When he came up for air, Abner suggested, "Let's call a girl over for you." He started to signal.

Sarah stopped him. "It's all right, Abner. Bray's taken a vow."

"Of celibacy?" he blurted. "Amidst a plenty of feminine pulchritude? Are you daft?"

"It's a temporary thing, I'm sure," Sarah replied for me.

"Did you strain yourself?" asked Abner grasping for understanding.

Sarah changed the subject. "Bray has something he wants to ask you."

Wicked Sarah, wicked woman! I could have shot her, but the cat was out of the bag.

"Sir . . . Abner," I spluttered, "May I have permission to pay court to your daughter?"

Abner's chair went over backwards, taking him and Maria to the floor. I jumped up, concerned that he might be injured, but found him laughing and Maria puzzled. I offered a hand up and had it accepted in a crushing grip.

"That'll be right fine," said Abner, "long as your intentions is honorable, even though you look to be twict her age. You got means, boy? Can you support her? You plannin' to settle down?"

We spent the evening drinking and getting to know each other better. His wife had died, and grief was the reason for him coming west. He'd headed for California with Alice Ann and her younger brother and stopped off in Arizona, liking the land along Sonoita Creek and seeing an opportunity. After a while, he and Maria headed upstairs.

"Maria is helping him with his grief," said Sarah sagely.

The next day, we searched the ore dumps we'd located and looked in vain around the old smelters.

In the heat of the day, Juan's voice wafted down the hillside. "I think I've found it."

I combed the hillside for some sign of him and found nothing.

Sarah approached. "Where is he?"

I shook my head as his call came again. Skirting a large thicket of manzanita, we ascended to where we thought his voice was calling. The "little apple" grew thick and ten feet tall, tangled until even hares avoided it.

Juan's voice came from the thicket. "It is here."

We twisted our way in following his voice. "This is why no one has found it before now."

I was elected to take a lump of ore to Captain Ewell, arriving as the sun set. Scientific devices, test tubes, retorts, crucibles, and such, items an assayer might use, filled the *cappen's* quarters.

"Yes, my own laboratory," chortled Ewell after dinner as he set to work testing my sample. "If it's platinum, it won't react with much, but it will dissolve in hot *agua regia*."

I didn't have to say anything.

"Royal water. A mixture of nitric acid and hydrochloric acid. Nasty stuff. It'll eat through most anything."

Hours later, he nodded. "Platinum all right, but I can help you no further than that."

"Can't you ship it for us with your ingots?" I asked. "And ours of silver and gold," I added.

"Nope," he replied. "It would cause us both too much unwanted attention."

"What do I do?"

"Refine it yourself," said Captain Ewell. "It's a small quantity, I gather. Separate it from the stone. Float the crushed stone off in a pan if you have to. Reduce its volume until you can carry it with you."

Riding back to Casa Blanca, I stopped by the Crumpton farm. Waving to Abner, I went in search of Alice Ann and found her tossing feed to hens. I wished her father had a porch swing and a porch to hang it on. Instead, I paid court whilst she fed the animals. It was wonderful!

In a smelly corral, watching carefully where we stepped, I bent down, and she kissed me.

Chapter 20 - Disasters

Juan Largo and I rode back to the ranch. We had been away too long. The San Rafael valley was a beautiful sea of grass, watered along its margins by clear, bubbling streams. A cattleman couldn't have asked for better except that he might wish it with fewer Apaches and to be closer to market.

"And without the bulls," said Juan Largo.

I looked at him. Had he read my mind? Had I been speaking aloud?

"I think," said Juan, "that I know why there are so many bulls, and why they are so ferocious."

Enigmatic as always I thought. Juan was no *duffer*, but he could be a *pilliock* at times for certain sure. I waited, knowing sooner or later that he would speak.

"The Apache," he said, "like to kill the calves and cows. Their meat is tenderer. They are more gentle and easier to slay."

I knew there was more. There had to be. I was pretty sure of this part of the story, but I wasn't going to give Juan the satisfaction of asking, so I pulled forth my *bacca* pouch and proceeded to stuff my nose-warmer. I'd shave my head and go east before I'd ask this *pilliock* to continue. Indians are comfortable with a long silence. They're good at it. Juan knew the white man's weakness: silence made him nervous. I'd kiss the *Tantarabobus*, hiz own self, and on the lips, too, before I gave in. I'd outlast the cunning old savage. There was no way I was going to ask Juan to continue.

"Juan," I said, "please, do go on. You've explained why there are so many bulls and so few cows. But, why are they so ferocious?"

Juan smiled. "I have already told you. They have no cows."

Killing him was not an option, but I could have done just then.

As we crossed the valley, we began looking for signs of our herd. We knew where the grass grew lushest. We knew where there was water and about how fast the cattle, left on their own, moved. They should have stayed bunched and wandered together from good grass to good grass. We found no strays. There was no sign of the herd. Finally, riding north and east, getting near our rancho, we began to see recently cropped grass. That seemed strange. The herd should have been further south and west along the fringes of the San Rafael. Juan and I were already well up into the Canelo Hills in sight of what were called the Mustang Mountains.

Following sign a few miles farther, we found where the cattle had been bunched and driven. There were many tracks close together beating down the grass like a road. Cattle had cropped the grass only along this narrow strip. This was an indication that the cattle were moving fast and not grazing. Among the marks of our cattle's passing, we found the occasional hoof print of a shod horse.

"See, here," said Juan. "It is not Indians driving the cattle. These men rode shod horses, and they are heading for the Cienega."

Rising near Sonoita Creek, the Cienega Creek, the little swamp, ran in the opposite direction, north toward Pantano Wash and Tucson. There were two markets for cattle. One was the army at the head of Sonoita Creek in Fort Buchanan and the other was Tucson.

"Let's follow the trail further," I said, "and be sure. Juan, how old is this trail?"

"Perhaps a week," he said, "maybe more."

"Then we can't catch up," I said. "Can we learn who has done this?"

"Perhaps in Tucson," Juan said after thought. "The herd has been sold, but maybe we can learn who sold it."

We gathered a few things at the ranch including the rest of our horses, and rode north following the trail. We arrived two days later. The heat and stink of too many people, too close together, who threw their garbage and chamber pots into the street nearly overcame us. The town was a huddle of poorly constructed adobes and *jacals*, houses made of sticks planted vertically in the ground side by side and covered with mud. It was hard to imagine a worse dwelling. Both types of building were without windows and had blankets in place of doors. Iron was hard to come by in this country, and the natives had never learned to use it for hinges whose screws didn't hold well in adobe. A proper door required lumber on top, sides, and bottom, and lumber, too, was scarce and expensive. There were some brave lads working a pinery in the Santa Ritas, despite Apache raids, but lumber remained scarce. The *paisanos*, the locals as they called themselves, didn't even use iron tires on their great wooden wheels. The streets were uneven drainage-ways full of litter and worse. It would be wrong to call it a one horse town. The old presidio, an adobe-walled fort built by the Spanish around 1750, ensured that there were at least four streets, one on each side and an interior plaza.

We located the butcher shop by the offal tossed in the street and by two hides bearing our brand hung in a nearby mesquite to dry.

Entering the shop, with Juan following, I pushed aside the door-blanket. The stench nearly floored me. It was as bad as the stench that rose from the former lines of the departed Mexican army the day after the Battle of Buena Vista. That was a horror I had not cared to encounter again. The stench of death, blood, and bowel mixed to roil the inner man, and I had trouble holding down my breakfast. The butcher was a middle aged Mexican with gray, stubbly jowls and a bloodstained apron.

"Don *Carnicero*," I said politely addressing him as sir butcher, "I am in the market for cattle. Do you know who might have some to sell?"

"Si," he responded, "Don Turco may still have a few. His men brought in a herd from Sonora last week."

Juan thanked him, and struggling for breath, we departed.

"Why doesn't he set up tables to conduct his trade outside?" I gasped.

"Perhaps," said Juan, "the thieves in this place have taught him that he is only safe indoors."

"Don Turco," I mused, "That will be Turk Pellewe, I think."

Juan nodded. "I think you are right."

Checking the loads on my pistols, I said, "Let's confront him."

"His friends are too many," replied Juan, "and we are too few."

Enumerating his legion of friends took the wind from my sails, but he was right. We agreed that there was no more to learn here and no feasible way to confront the Pellewes, Helligans, their too numerous banditos, plus their partner Robinson, at least not with guns. Every moment we remained there was risk of being noticed, so as we turned our mounts to the south toward Tubac and the road to the Casa Blanca. I felt defeated. I wanted to fight but was outnumbered worse than General Taylor at Buena Vista after President Polk took away most of his army.

At the Crumpton farm on Sonoita Creek, I stopped to talk to Abner. Across the field, I saw Alice Ann talking to a man in a fine suit. He took her hand and held it.

With growing heat, I demanded of Abner to know who that was.

"Don Hombre," interjected Juan, "calm yourself."

Recognizing Palatine Robinson, I glared at Juan and turned to Abner. "What's he doing here?"

"He's paying court to my daughter," said Abner. "I know I told you that you could, but he has lots of money and will take good care of her, let her live well. He's a gentleman, that one. And I owe him money. I lost to him at cards, and he said he'd never try to collect a debt from his father-in-law."

I stammered, "His father-in. . .his *gaffer?* More like . . .debt."

"I owe him a lot."

Angrier than I had ever been, I broke loose of Juan's grasp and turned my horse toward Robinson. He turned, hearing, I thought, the sound of galloping hooves. He went for his pistol, but I leapt from the dashing roan and landed on him. Rising, heedless of his gun, I lifted him with my left arm and beat his head with my right.

Alice screamed.

I released him, allowing Robinson to fall as I caught breath and reached back for a more powerful punch. Alice grabbed my arm.

"Don't," she pleaded. "My father has given him permission to pay court, and he is kind and gentlemanly."

Seated on the ground, the gentleman in question tried again to pull his weapon. My arm still impeded by Alice Ann, I kicked it from his hand. She, I thought, saw only that I kicked him and wailed anew.

Breaking loose of her, I again raised him from the ground and releasing him, pummeled him left-right-left. Blood spurted from his nose and lips. One eye was swelling shut as he dropped out of range, and I circled. Alice threw her body over his to protect him.

"You're evil!" she screamed at me. "And brutal! And awful. No gentleman. You are just a wild beast of the frontier! I never want to see you again."

"But, Alice . . ." I stammered.

"Never!" she said her voice ice. Her arm extended, finger pointing me away.

I wasn't done with Palatine, but I knew he had licked me in the fight that mattered. Mounting my roan, I signaled to Juan and rode off toward Casa Blanca, my heart broken.

"Don Hombre, you have brought the fight into the open. Now Señor Robinson knows you do not like him. He will see in this the rejection of his partnership offers and take stronger measures. When we needed to be smart, you used brute strength. And you didn't kill him. You should have when he reached for his *pistole*. It would have been better. You have many enemies and few friends. Even the señorita doesn't like you anymore."

My cattle were gone. The rustlers had stolen most of my horses. Outlaws were threatening my friends. And my beautiful *piskie* princess was seeing a man I knew to be a slaver and who I was pretty sure was married. What would become of Alice Ann? What plans did he have for her? What price would she bring in a Mexican bordello? Why should I care? She had rejected me for money and a pretty suit.

Was she fickle? Did I love her, or was she just a passing fancy? Oh, I was *piskie-led.* I didn't care. I still wanted her. She was beautiful and innocent and pure. I was uncertain if she had any qualities of character. Was she strong-willed? Was she tough? Could she think for herself? I didn't know. I only knew I wanted her.

Chapter 21 - It Gets Worse

"Go to her, Bray," insisted Sarah. "She loves you. She'll forgive you, or she isn't worth having." Western soaked my still raw fists in a mixture of herbs and wrapped them. It had been a short fight, but I hadn't held anything back.

Three days after the fight, I was still drinking with little else to do. I'd been drinking nasty cactus whiskey, and it gives a man a strange feeling, mean and sorry for himself at the same time. Why shouldn't I feel sorry for myself? I thought. My herd was gone, taken by men too numerous to pursue. My girl was gone, taken by a married man who could have no honest plan for her future, she accepting him partly out of loyalty to a father who owed him money. And my friends and I were about to be driven out of Arizona.

"Leave me be," I mumbled. "Don't pester a blind man."

"Blind!" exclaimed Sarah. "Is there some injury I missed?"

"Only to my heart," I replied. "And I plan to ease the suffering by drinking cactus juice until I go blind." I took a long pull on the bottle. "Shouldn't take long with this stuff."

I don't remember much after that. Sarah complained of cleaning up some mess I'd made, and Juan that I was gaining weight. I awoke in Guadalupe's bed feeling her warm smooth skin but in no condition to do anything about it and no mood. My head throbbed, and my belly rebelled. I rose and, pulling my long shirt over my head, stumbled down the stairs and out the back to relieve myself of cactus juice by every means imaginable. Then I headed back inside to retrieve the rest of my clothing and splash some water in my face from the basin. My mouth needed rinsing as well, and the place where I sat was hotter than chili peppers.

I stripped off the shirt again so as not to get it wet and found myself embraced tightly by a very pleasing and very naked Guadalupe.

"Who threw me in bed with this girl?" I roared. "Juan, I'll kill you! She deserves better."

I lost my balance, much befuddled by too much tequila for too long a time, and sat heavily on the girl's bed pulling her with me and holding her tight. Then I began to sob into her hair, her jet-black hair that smelled of cinnamon, cloves and chocolate, crying on her shoulder. She smelled wonderfully of chili, onions, garlic, and cheap perfume. I stroked her shoulder, then her bosom. She stroked my back and hip. I wasn't up to more.

Rising, she helped me dress. Downstairs, Sarah was making my breakfast of greasy bacon, eggs poached in chili, and excellent bread. I greeted her with a grunt and sat heavily. She placed the plate before me, and I rose, suddenly overcome, and rushed out the back door to rid myself of green bile and sour tequila. It was another full day before I could tolerate food, but I was on the mend.

I don't know why I should have been, but I was. Nothing was resolved. I didn't know how I felt about Alice Ann. I was a pauper, and my cattle were gone. Sarah was about to be driven out of business. But Sarah loved me as a friend. Juan thought of me as friend and something special. Guadalupe loved me. With this much love, how could I not feel better? They needed me to be better. Even Alice Ann needed me, although she didn't know it. I would save her from herself even if she rejected me. So what? Guadalupe still loved me.

"There is nothing," said Juan Largo sagely, "like a naked woman to remind a man that he is a man."

"Indeed." Sarah nodded.

"Yer daft," I grumbled.

That afternoon Moses Carson showed up at Casa Blanca. Some men just naturally arrive at the scene when they sense that bad trouble is brewing. Old Mose was one of them. I'd met him before in Santa Fe. Kit's older half-brother, he stood over six feet tall with grizzled hair and shoulders wide as a doorway. He was scarred, three-fingered, gap-toothed, and one-eyed in his sixties but still monstrously strong and able, a fighter. He wore a buckskin war shirt complete with clumps of hair he said were scalps he'd taken. Below he had on greasy, Mexican pantaloons with concho-buttons up the side of the leg, his shins covered knee-high moccasins. He smelled of brain-tanned hide, pemmican, and tobacco.

He swaggered in to Sarah Bowman's Casa Blanca, adjusting his eye-patch, calling out to Sarah and me, "Howdy, neighbors! When's the fight begin?"

That was Mose. He could smell a fight brewing from miles away.

"Hi, Mose," I replied. "Fight is our affair. We can't pull you in nor risk your life, and the risk is high."

Sarah agreed.

Mose looked downcast. "Have pity on an old man who has lived a sinful life. There'll be a fight, and I'll be in it. I can't be fightin' fer the Helligans. My onliest chanct of heaven is to fight on the side of the angels before I die."

"Sorry, Mose," I said. "I'm not even sure there'll be a fight. We are badly outgunned."

"Have a drink with me," said Mose happily. "Perhaps Sarah has a bottle of Dutch Courage lying about, and we can share it before we clean out that nest of rattlers in Tucson."

"He can't drink," pronounced Sarah flatly. Then she smiled. "But I'll have one with you."

The sun was setting, when 10-year-old Joshua Crumpton rushed into the room. "Father has given her to him! Robinson has taken Alice Ann to Tucson to prepare for the wedding!"

"But," I gasped, "he's already married and can't wed again!"

"I know," said Joshua. "That's why I came."

"Told you there'd be a fight," exulted Mose.

"Tomorrow," I said, "in the morning, we'll call in Graydon and make a plan. Sarah, me, Mose, Juan Largo. . ." I looked at him and he nodded and rose leaving his young lady of the moment to limp across the room and join us. "And perhaps Graydon. Good fighters all, but not much of an army against 15 or 20 gun-hands."

Having thus explained the hopelessness of our situation, I retired for the evening professing to still be feeling the effects of too much cactus whiskey. After midnight, I arose and walked quietly down the stairs and out to the corral where I saddled my horse. I checked my weapons, two Hawken rifles, Walker Colt, two Dragoon Colts, Bowie, and 'hawk. That meant I had fourteen shots before I'd have to reload. I guessed I'd have to take out the last six with knife and axe. I was angry, cold, killing angry, but I would not risk my friends' lives.

Cactus whiskey can leave a man like that, not caring if he lives of dies but hell-bent on a higher purpose and full of nobility. I figured I had to protect everyone, even from themselves, and this whole mess was my fault. It started when I killed a bad man in Santa Fe. It got worse when I struck a nasty weasel that was horning in on my precious maiden and my friend's business. I had screwed it all up. Our predicament was my fault, and I needed to fix it or die trying. It was the dragoon way. I was proud of being a dragoon and of what I'd learned as a soldier. A dragoon never let his comrades down and always protected the weak. That's what Captain Ewell had taught.

Realization struck me. Was I risking Alice Ann's life? Maybe. But there was no other way. Maybe one man could get in and out quietly, stealing the girl away without arousing her captors. What awaited her was a fate worse than death. Robinson couldn't marry her. He might keep her as a mistress for a while, but sooner or later his wife would find out, and he would sell Alice Ann to a bordello deep in Mexico.

I led the horse for half a mile before I mounted and rode my strawberry roan north toward Tucson. The summer night was cold but not nearly as cold as the icy anger in my heart. The night was moonless and dark as my soul. It was a two days' ride to the old presidio, if I pressed my horse hard. I would ride through the night resting toward morning. Traveling by night would not get me there any sooner. I must wait for darkness to attack, but I would have a few daylight hours to reconnoiter.

Sombrero pulled low on my brow to shade and hide my face and serape hiding my weapons, I hoped they would be disguise enough as I worked my way around town. I stopped at vendor stalls buying things to eat and drink while watching, moving slowly, and asking discrete questions. Robinson had a large, two-story house north of the presidio walls. The Helligans had a few adobes scattered around a corral to the west. They were close but did not share a compound. That was luck.

I studied Robinson's hacienda for hours, watching the comings and goings and searching for any sign of Alice Ann. The house had porches on both floors and single-story wings on the sides, like arms without. These seemed to be servants' quarters, kitchen, and storage. A wall with a *zaguan*, a gate large enough to admit a wagon, closed the front. I never saw Alice Ann, but it seemed to me she was being kept in a second floor room. A tailor carrying bolts of cloth went in and emerged later. At sunset, a dinner was taken in. All of the rooms had access from the outside. I couldn't tell if they connected within.

As the dusk began to deepen, men began to arrive singly and in pairs. Palatine greeted and welcomed them to his home. I counted eight entering what appeared to be a *sala*, a large room, on the first floor. Eight was better than twenty. I slipped away to wait for the early morning hours when all should be sleeping.

Chapter 22 - The Rescue of Alice Ann

One man alone stands little chance against an army, though one man stands a better chance of moving unseen and unheard through the night. Alice Ann's room must be locked to keep her from coming forth and meeting Robinson's wife, I thought. Perhaps they had met and Alice was now Robinson's prisoner, though I saw no guard on the door. It might be locked. If locked, how was I to open it without arousing the household? Once I broke open the door, there was no one to watch our backs as we fled. The mission was hopeless.

I returned well after midnight. The distant stars were cold giving no light on a night dark as a *crow's*, that is to say a witch's, heart. I was *thrown kiting* over this and that lying about in the *tulgy* night as if I were *durk, durk* as a bat. *Afeard* I was, *afeard* of failing my Alice Ann. A cold hand closed about *me* heart. *Danted* I was, but determined to continue. I ached for her, as I never had for any woman. Juan would have called this foolishness since she was too young to know her own heart and mind. Sarah was more *romantical*. She believed in love at first sight and living happily ever after.

Arriving by Palatine Robinson's wall, I looked over and saw light still issuing from his sala, his hall, the door open to admit the cool night air and release the heavy pong of *bacca* and the sound of laughter from his assembled guests. I had hoped they would be gone and was awarded only second best. They were drunk. Or so they seemed. Perhaps their noise would cover the crash of breaking down the door.

A sound touched me ear, a small sound, no louder than a mouse coughing or a pebble rolling. The hair stood up along my spine. Certain they had posted a guard, I slipped away from the wall into darker shadows. The smooth sound of a snake on sand came from the night. I knew that sound. It was a revolver being drawn. Still I could see nothing. Unwilling to make a sound, my heart and breath stood still. Click-clack. It seemed loud as the bells of St. Andrew's *kirk*. The pistol had been cocked. Still I was *durk*. I searched the night for the gunman.

"Turn around," said a cold voice from the dark. "Walk away from the house." The voice was high pitched but brooked no argument. It was the voice of a man used to being obeyed and who would allow no other option. Somewhere nearby, a man pulled back the blanket that covered a doorway emitting a little light as he spat into the street. Briefly light *gliddered* off the bald pate of the gunman.

We walked away from town into the surrounding desert. I cast about for a way to render the gunman disarmed, but it was all I could do to avoid the sharp brambles of the cacti and other things that grew about. One hundred paces I counted, then two hundred. Soon, soon he would kill me and leave me far enough from town that I would not be discovered until morning when the vultures gathered for a feast. Worse, I was failing Alice Ann.

Vague shapes formed ahead. Saguaro perhaps, I thought, but not so tall, and more solid than the common *stickery-stuff*. Soon, I must act soon, or I was dead.

One of the dark shapes spoke in Sarah Bowman's voice. "Do you have him?"

"I do," said a higher pitched voice I recognized now as belonging to Captain Richard Ewell. It came from behind me.

"Great Western!" I exclaimed, "What are you doing here?"

The flame-haired Amazon responded, "I come to save you, though I don't know why and I've brought Juan Largo and Paddy Graydon besides, and Old Mose to boot."

"I can't risk your lives," I insisted, "on a personal quest."

"Ain't yur call, chil'," said Moses Carson, and the others agreed.

"Waste no more time," said Ewell. "Tell us what you know."

I explained the results of my reconnaissance.

Ewell thought a minute. "I shall general this thing with your permission." All assented. "Good. Sarah, you and Bray go and fetch the girl. Bray, give your rifles and one pistol to Juan. He and Mose will stay near the gate with me and cover the entrance to the gambling hall, shooting anyone foolish enough to emerge. Paddy and I will guard the street watching for the approach of reinforcements. We are the reserve, able to respond to emergencies. Any questions?

"Good," he continued, "and remember one thing: no plan survives contact with the enemy. We must respond as the situation changes. I will be near the gate where I can observe the battle."

We approached the house again where light still came from the sala where the gathering within continued unabated. There was no good way to cross the courtyard. We might encounter servants coming from the kitchens.

Climbing over the roof might arouse even more suspicion. So we walked arm-in-arm across the yard, trying to look like we belonged therc, hoping that with guests in the house, we might be mistaken for those legitimately present.

We made our way quietly up the stairs to the room I thought might be where Palatine kept Alice. Sarah stood watch. The door was locked as I'd feared. The doorframe was soft cottonwood. Not having a key there was nothing for it, but to break it down. The soft wood splintered under my assault with less noise than you might guess. Nonetheless, it was enough to wake Alice.

"Who is there!" she yelped as I leapt into the room placing my hand over her mouth to silence her. She bit me.

"Alice, it's me." I said. "Hurry, we must get you dressed and out of here before someone comes."

"Why would I leave?" the girl asked.

"You're a prisoner," I stammered. "The door was locked from outside."

"Palatine," she said, "told me it was necessary to keep me safe in the city."

"He was holding you prisoner!" I insisted.

"We are to be wed," she replied.

Startled, I said, "But he's already married. Haven't you met his wife? She's exceptionally pretty."

"He has no wife," she said. "Leave or I will scream."

"He does!" I hissed. "We must go."

She started to scream. Before I could do anything Sarah was all over us, pinning the girl and telling me to tear up the bed sheets. I did. Sarah bound and gagged her in a trice.

"I hope no one heard that," I said.

Sarah replied, "We've got to go."

Alice struggled as I led her to the stairs, so I threw her over my shoulder where she managed to knock into things and make quite a bit of noise. I stumbled on the wooden stairs and Sarah grabbed us both, but the stairs rang hollow seeming loud in my ears. Around her gag, Alice managed a strangled yelp.

In the sala, someone said, "Did you hear something? There was a noise."

Another voice replied, "You'd better check."

We ran, Alice still over my shoulder, Sarah behind. Someone emerging from the sala blocked its light for a moment. "Hey, you there! Stop!"

Another voice called, "They're kidnapping the girl!"

Then a rifle roared shooting blinding flame across the courtyard, and I heard a body drop. Somewhere in the night, Old Mose chortled as Juan Largo raised my Walker Colt and fired. There was another roar and flash of flame as another body dropped. Then we were across the court.

From down the street in the direction of Helligans' adobes, there was shouting. We'd roused the town. Mose fired again.

From within the sala, there was noise and shouting. A few shots emerged, but those firing were night-blind from their own lights.

"Put out the lights!" And the light in the sala winked to darkness.

"Get out there!"

"You go," came the reply.

"They can't see you now."

Juan's pistol roared again, but the shot did not take effect. He and Mose were almost as blind as those within.

"We're trapped," came a voice from the house.

"See if the back door is covered!" That was bad news. We had to go. Mose and Juan could keep them bottled up only a little longer. My two friends did not have many shots left. Paddy fired down the street at something.

"Damn!" I heard someone cry from the direction he'd fired.

"Time to go," said Ewell. "Get her to the horses. We'll cover your retreat."

I tossed Alice Ann across a horse and tied her down as she struggled, and Sarah mounted. Not far off, I could hear Ewell directing his battle. Juan and Mose fell back, and then as they fired a volley, Paddy and Ewell leapfrogged passed them. Soon, we were all mounted and riding hard toward Tubac.

Chapter 23 - Flight to Tubac

We arrived at Canoa ranch with the dawn chewing on trail dust and stinking of horse sweat.

Ewell looked over our lathered stock. "We've got to stop, feed the stock, and give them time to rest."

"We can't," said Sarah flatly. "They'll be right behind us."

"Maybe not," replied Juan Largo. "It took them time to get their horses saddled. By then, we had disappeared into the night. They would have waited till morning to search for our trail. Around the town, where the trails are hard packed, this will not be easy."

"Aye, laddies," said Paddy, "and ifn they recognized us, which they did for certain sure, they'll look along the road to Fort Buchanan first."

"'Sides," opined Mose, "it's time fer my breakfast, and they make good food here."

Canoa ranch functioned as a stage station on the road from Tucson to Tubac and Sonoita Creek. The road went almost straight across the Santa Ritas from Tubac to Johnny Ward's ranch on the creek. Canoa was also an inn that served pretty good food whipped up by a couple of Down-Easters from Maine.

A few miles out of Tucson, we'd halted and let Alice Ann ride upright. At Canoa, I helped her down and removed her gag.

She immediately started screaming. "Help, someone! I'm being kidnapped! They pulled me from the arms of my fiancé! Help! Please, someone, anyone."

The Down-Easters emerged from the inn armed with pistols and dark looks, but recognizing those in the party, they relaxed and smiled. "Good joke. But be careful you don't get shot."

"It's no joke!" screamed Alice.

They laughed and turned back to the house. "We won't be tooken in. Breakfast will be ready soon."

A beautiful woman emerged wearing a look of great concern. After all, a sister was in danger.

"Oh, it's her!" said Mrs. Elvira Robinson, who many thought the most beautiful woman in Arizona. Hers was a more mature, more classical beauty than Alice Ann's, not quite so fairy-like. She turned on her heal.

"Who was that?" asked Alice.

"Your rival for Palatine's affections," I replied.

"I have no rival. He swears he loves only me, and I've never seen her before."

I motioned to Sarah to look after Alice Ann and took off after Palatine's wife, Elvira. I caught up with her in the dining room.

"Mrs. Robinson, may I have a word?"

She looked at me as if I were a puddle of nauseating offal left too long in the sun. Even her nose twitched as if detecting a foul odor. "What? What new devilment has Palatine dreamed up for his henchmen to visit on me? Isn't banishment to this place enough?"

My mind worked fast. She thought me a henchman. Perhaps I could use that. Banished here? No wonder Alice Ann hadn't seen her. She seemed more annoyed with Alice than with Palatine. Perhaps she thought the banishment only a temporary annoyance while her husband prepared the child for her new life in Mexican bondage.

I played a hunch. "We're taking the girl to Mexico."

"Oh good," she said. "Perhaps I can return to my home soon. I don't know why he had to wine and dine her. He should have just shipped her off."

"He wanted her to go willingly and not cause a spectacle," I said. Kidnapping white women was hard on one's reputation.

She humpfed. "Well, she's causing one now."

"I don't like to admit it," I said, "but I'm terrible at remembering names, especially Mexican names. I remember that we're supposed to go to Santa Cruz, but what is the name of the contact there? Something '-ez'."

"Rodriguez, Rudolfo Rodriguez," she replied. "You'll find some of his men at the cantina."

"Thank you, ma'am." Es or ez at the end of a name is the Mexican equivalent of son on an English name or -s on a Welsh one. Lots of names end that way.

"Are you carrying the guns, as well?" she asked. "I didn't see any pack animals."

"No," I said, "we're not."

She came close and whispered. "He must be supplying the Apaches first. Don't breathe a word of that to Rodriguez. He can't be allowed to know."

"Yes, ma'am. Excuse me now."

I hastened out to talk to my friends and explain the situation.

"I'd be surprised if she didn't recognize me," said Ewell. "I'm well known in Tucson, but known in uniform. Mrs. Robinson must have focused on the girl."

I nodded. "She may have seen some of us and think we're in his employ. But getting near her and talking near her are a risk."

"What can we do?" asked Paddy.

Sarah spoke first. "Stay out here with the stock. Tend to them. Let Juan go in and return with some food for breakfast and the trail. We'll push on to Tubac."

"It'll be hard on the stock," said Ewell.

"I don't see an alternative," I replied. We were gone in 30 minutes without an incident.

Tubac was one of the largest and most important cities in Arizona and the first to have a newspaper. As we came over the last hill, we gazed down on two rows of adobe casas baking in the sun with a crumbling *iglesia*, church, and presidio at the distant end. Charles Poston had brought the abandoned town back to life. It was headquarters for his mining interests, which lay to the east in the Santa Ritas and west about twenty miles away.

"We have to stop," said Juan, "and rest the stock."

Ewell nodded. "But there is no law and no militia. If they want us, they can take us, and others might get hurt if we make a fight here."

"They'll hesitate," said Sarah, "to murder us in front of witnesses."

Alice Ann spoke. "Not if I tell them you kidnapped me! Let me go!"

"Juan," I asked, "do you think the stock can make it to the Hacienda Santa Rita? We could make a stand there on ground that would favor us."

"Maybe, more likely not," said Manso Apache Juan Largo.

Ewell spoke. "Poston depends on me to protect his people. Perhaps he will trade us for fresh mounts."

Poston did have fresh mounts for us and news. "The dragoons will be moving up to Fort Breckinridge soon," he said. "That will be too far away. We'll have trouble with the Apache. Infantry will be no help, so I'm organizing a militia. They'll be Arizona Rangers, like the Texas Rangers, whose job will be to protect us from the Apache. Bray, I want you to join."

"I'll give some consideration," I responded, thinking that I had troubles and commitments enough without adding another one.

Poston looked me in the eye. "See that you do." The man had a way of getting others to do his bidding.

We rode with Ewell as far as Fort Buchanan. The Helligans never caught up.

At the fort, Captain Richard Ewell, post commander, received two sets of orders. The first directed him to report to the military post at Magoffinsville, Texas, later known as Fort Bliss, near El Paso, for court martial duty. The second called for him to transfer his command to Fort Breckenridge 100 miles to the north on the San Pedro River. In October, the Army planned to replace two companies of the 1st Dragoons with two of companies of the 7th Infantry. Ewell was leaving us.

"You're still in danger," he said in parting. "Robinson and the Helligans can ambush you at any time or follow through on their threats to your businesses. With the dragoons away, the Apache will play." He wheezed his strange laugh at his *bon mott*. "Since these renegades are supplying the Indians with rifles, it could become very heated."

The only good news was that Sarah was finally getting through to Alice. She was finally becoming suspicious of Palatine Robinson's intentions. At least, I hoped, we wouldn't need to worry about the girl running away back to Tucson. She still wouldn’t look at me or talk to me.

Chapter 24 - The Arizona Rangers

Juan Largo looked appealingly to the Great Western and then across the corner table where we sat in the smoky *sala*, main room, of the Casa Blanca. "*Patron*, you can't stay here and do nothing forever. We got to get back to the rancho."

"Why?" I asked. "As you'll recall *backalong* the Helligans already *reeved* me *beeves*. There *be* naught there to tend."

Sarah Bowman, the Great Western, mistress of the Casa Blanca, an establishment renowned as the finest of its sort in all Arizona, a boast stretching from Patagonia to Sonoita Creek to Tubac and Tucson, grabbed me under the chin and forced me to look into her sky-blue eyes. "Then go see your fairy queen, Miss Alice Ann, before she runs off to Palatine Robinson again."

I pulled my head back out of her powerful grasp. "She made it *clar aniff*, she don' want me. She *runned* off *afore*. She wants her fancy-man, Palatine."

"She's a mere girl and doesn't know her own mind, you blamed Cornishman." Sarah towered over six feet tall with flame-red hair and a temper to match. "Owen Bray St. Gnomebrey, you need to go see her."

Guadalupe approached our table and began to rub my neck from behind. She was a beauty and it felt good, but *me* heart *yarned* for *me piskie-maid* who had cast me off. "Come on, Hombre, I take you upstairs."

The invitation was tempting and part of my body wanted to go with her, but my heart just wasn't in it. I adjusted myself more comfortably in my chair.

"Not now, *luv*," I replied unable to get my mind off Alice Ann who had cast me off. Turning to Apache Juan Largo, I said, "We need to stay here and protect Great Western and her girls. Have you forgotten the Helligans want her business? Or that we've angered them exceedingly?"

"The Great Western can protect herself!" roared Sarah. Startled, her girls produced pistols hidden in folds of their clothing and one of the guard-girls from the roof came running down the stairs, rifle held foremost, to see what was wrong.

"Sarah," I said, "*Ye* are indeed the Great Western, but Ewell is gone, and you can't depend on Paddy Graydon to come to your aid."

Sarah tossed her hair great red mane flying. "I got along fine before Paddy Graydon ever came into my life."

Juan, not to be dissuaded, said, "Then, Don Hombre, we should go trade with the Chiricahua. You always like that."

"They make me nervous and give me the *collywobbles*."

I knew we should go trade. An idea was growing in the back of my mind, but unwilling to let me see it. The Helligans and Robinson traded with bands of the Apache hostile to both the Arizona settlements and the Chiricahua and with the Mexicans equally as hostile. Perhaps trade with the Chiricahua could be turned to making three already distrustful groups, Coyotero, Mexican, and Helligans, hostile to each other into enemies instead of wary traders. But there the idea hid behind the curtains of my mind and stubbornly refused to reveal itself.

Weeks had passed and *piskie* Alice Ann didn't run away from her father's door, but she wasn't speaking to me neither. We'd rescued her from Palatine Robinson who would have sold her into slavery. We couldn't convince her that Palatine already had a wife. Women! Go figure. Juan and I camped at the Casa Blanca. Robinson and the Helligans remained quiet, perhaps consumed by their trading activities of offering guns to Mexicans and Indians. By 1860, every civic leader of any standing in Sonora and Chihuahua was plotting revolt and needed guns. The Tonto and Coyotero Apache, having guns for the first time, were using settlers for target practice. Fortunately, chewing bullets into shape didn't make for very accurate shooting. The Apache didn't melt or mold their lead.

"Faint heart never won maiden fair," said Sarah with finality.

Realizing she left me no choice, I said, "All right. I'll go visit Alice Ann."

Riding down the canyon from the Casa Blanca at Patagonia, which is to say, the Mowry Mine, I daydreamed about the *piskie* princess the entire way. Arriving at Sonoita Creek, I spied her working in her father's gardens. Espying me, she turned and walked swiftly toward her father's *adobe casa*. Fearing she might get there before I could talk to her, I sent my horse flying over the fence and sliding to a halt at her feet.

"Alice Ann, *me fairie* queen, *me piskie* maiden . . ."

"Humph!" said Alice Ann.

"Alice Ann, *me luv* . . ."

She crossed her arms and turned away. Cold, corpse cold, her love dead. "I have no wish to speak to you, kidnapper." Icicles clung to the last.

Blind, deaf, and dumb, I rode away from her, unaware of my surroundings and only sure I did not wish to be near friends at the Casa Blanca. I cannot say how long I rode, perhaps through the night. Two rifle shots brought me round.

A knot of men stood on the banks of the Santa Cruz River while two others faced each other at 50 paces. Bang, bang! They fired once again and began to reload their Burnside Rifles with paper cartridges.

Recognizing a man, I knew in the knot, I rode up to Charles Poston and dismounted. "*Ahoy* Poston, what *betides*?" We shook hands though mine almost slid from his smooth, seemingly greasy hands. I checked to ensure I still had all my digits.

"You know them both," said he. "There stands Sylvester Mowry, late officer of the U.S. Army and current representative from Arizona to the Congress to plead that we be made a separate judicial district. Yonder stands Edward Cross, our newspaper editor, who proclaims that Arizona should be a territory. The pair caused uncomplimentary things to be said of each other in Cross's paper, and Mowry, being Mowry, issued a challenge." Bang! Bang!

"How can they miss at this range?" I asked stunned.

"I know not."

We stood near the river on the cultivated land east of the town. The main street ran north to south beginning at the church and Poston's house, passing the old presidio, and running between crumbling, featureless adobe blocks referred to as *casas* and stores.

Bang! went Cross's rifle. Click went Mowry's, a misfire.

"Mr. Mowry, it is agreed you should reload as you have a shot coming." Cross stood up straight, rifle at his side, ready to accept his fate.

"I will not fire at an unarmed man," proclaimed Mowry. "I consider honor satisfied."

The pair apologized to each other for the things they'd caused to be printed and signed a joint statement of apology to be published in Cross's newspaper. I wondered if Cross charged Mowry for his half of the printing.

"So," said Poston, "What brings you to Tubac?"

"I wish to join the Foreign Legion."

"We've no Foreign Legion here, but the Arizona Rangers," said Poston, "are looking for a few good men. You provide your own rifle, pistols, knife, tomahawk, ammunition, horse, and tack. We'll provide a few rations and all the Apaches you can stomach."

Poston introduced me to the officers. Tevis was young and handsome and given to bragging about his exploits. Jack Swilling, with mustaches hanging well below his chin, was one of the funniest and bravest men I ever met. He had swagger to be sure, and he told some whoppers.

"I hear you want to join the Foreign Legion," said Swilling. "Welcome to the Arizona Rangers. The idea is that we'll be like the Texas Rangers and operate in small companies against Indians and outlaws, and if needed, serving as judge, jury, and executioner. There's not much point in taking prisoners since there's no way to try them in court. Don't worry too much. Indians first. With the dragoons gone to Fort Breckinridge, they'll give us enough trouble."

Chapter 25 - Scout

Thwang! A bullet struck the rock above my head and ricocheted off into space stinging my face with granite chips.

Beside me Tevis hunched down low, trying to become one with the rock. "Ole Mose told me to reload as soon as you fire your pistol, don't wait and fire all six. Always have six ready for them. That time we went hunting together up along the Hi-lay River, we kilt 22 'Paches that way."

Ole Mose who hung around Tubac and Sonoita Creek. Jim Tevis, lieutenant of the Arizona Rangers, talked too much. He was the hero of too many of his far-fetched stories. Just like a lieutenant, I thought, trying to prove his worth to the men not realizing that he already had done so just by sticking to the trail.

"Owen, see that one moving up. Get him with your rifle." He wouldn't call me Bray since my enlistment papers said Owen Bray.

"He's out of range even for my sweet Hawken, *cappen*," I replied. "And he knows it, or we shouldn't be seeing the heathen *Tantarabobus*."

It was a standoff into its second day. We had a grand position, a wee crawl space big enough for two under some tumbled boulders with a grand view of the San Pedro Valley. The lieutenant's horse lay dead behind us at the head of a rocky alcove. It fell carrying Tevis to the last with an arrow through its lights. Mine had hung on in the cove for most of a day until mad with thirst it had charged downhill through the Apache to a stream a mile away. Just a few steps away we could see and smell the lieutenant's dead horse out our "backdoor." Above us was a space where we could crawl up to the "roof" unobserved. It seemed there was only one way into the cove, and we had that covered. A bush obscured the downhill entrance, so the Aravaipa Apaches weren't quite sure where we were hiding.

"We'll be okay," said Tevis, reassuring himself.

"We'll be just fine, cap'n," I replied. "We've a nice breeze comes through to keep us cool and a fine roof *or'ed* to keep us dry. If we just had a wee bit more water, we'd be in paradise. Might make it yet with or without the water."

"I could try for my canteen from the horse."

I looked at him. "Yes, and you might make it back alive. They've shooters in the rocks high above this cove as well as those out front. The ones above will get you. Should have brought it and your ammunition with you when we ducked in here. No use to it."

"Captain Jack will be here with the troop soon," he insisted. "Swilling won't let us down."

"Aye. And we've sure done our jobs as scouts, haven't we?"

Tevis looked at me quizzically.

I told him, "A scout's job is to find more trouble than he can handle by himself, hang onto it, and wait for the troop to come up. We've certainly done that. And all would be fine with the world if the troop just knew where we were and if we had a wee bit o' water."

"We had to come this way!" said Tevis defending his actions.

"And so we did. There were Apaches in every other direction."

No use needling him. He'd failed to grab powder and shot and his canteen from the saddle, but there was no helping it now.

The Rangers spent almost as much time at home as in the field. There wasn't much in the way of pay, but the Rangers provided food and ammunition for field operations. Arizona, not having any government, had no way to raise money to pay us, so we'd stay at home until the Apache, Aravaipas, Pinals, and Coyoteros, raided someone's farm or gold mine. The Chiricahuas hadn't caused many problems as yet. They stole a few head of stock now and then but generally left us alone. There would be a raid, and then we'd be out after the heathen and pursue them until we'd made them hurt. That way they learned to pick easier targets like Mexicans in Sonora and unwary travelers on the Southern Immigrant Trail that ran up the San Pedro Valley and over to Tucson.

The day was dry and thirsty, but fortunately a cool breeze blew. We were in a space under a big boulder wide enough for two men to crawl abreast from one end to the other, about 15 feet. It wasn't more than two feet high except where an opening above our heads led up to the top of the boulder, our roof. If you crawled up there and were careful, lying on your stomach, you could snake around covered by the surrounding boulders and get a view of the countryside, south and north but not west toward the river. In our shelter, I looked down the only possible lane of approach, down a hill that sloped steeply to the west.

An Apache moved. Tevis banged off two shots from his Colt and reached for my flask to reload. It was wasted powder and shot, and I wanted to stop him. I consoled myself that it let the Indians know we weren't sleeping and might be heard by those coming to relieve us. They'd be down on the river trying to pick up our trail, ten miles away. The lieutenant reached for my caps to finish the job of loading.

Tevis was ready for a fight. "Do you think they'll rush us?"

"Why should they?" I replied. "They know we haven't much water. Another day and we might ask them to kill us as a kindness." My canteen had been empty since dawn and the headaches and cramps had begun that come when there's no water. "If they rush us, someone might get hurt. They'll bide their time a bit."

The breeze dropped, and the stink of the dead horse became unbearable. Nervous, Tevis moved about. He crawled up to the "roof" for a better look around. A large boulder blocked part of the view to the west. It and its brothers formed a low, unclimbable ridge. To the south our ridge dropped away into a steep cliff and arroyo. The arroyos in this direction offered a concealed line of approach for an army but allowed no direct access to our position. The back of our cove rose into more cliffs. To the north, the mountain rose straight up for hundreds of feet. From my position I could only see west along the spur down the hill to the stream.

"They're above us on the north way up on the cliffs," Tevis whispered from above hoarse with thirst, his lips cracked and blackened.

I heard him move above and the thud as his boots struck ground by our back door. Two rifles cracked from far above. I turned to look as Tevis ran for his horse. Judging a steep downward shot is difficult. The Apaches missed. Rifles were slow to reload and soon arrows flew, but Tevis had his saddle bags, powder flask, and canteen. He ran and dove for our position sliding in as an arrow pierced his leg. He grinned, and I pulled him in.

Our lieutenant was brave enough if foolhardy and a braggart. We sipped water and ate food from his bags greedily. The arrow could wait. It would still be there after dinner.

The arrow required both of our attention. The Apaches used hollow reeds with a detachable, hardwood fore shaft to which an iron arrowhead fashioned from a barrel hoop was bound. Some Army general order required that barrel hoops be accounted for and collected. It wasn't to account for the contents of the barrels. It was to keep the hoops from falling into Indian hands.

The tip protruded slightly through the skin of his ankle. With one swift, though painful to him, motion I pushed it all the way through and pulled loose the fore shaft. Suction made withdrawing the reed shaft more difficult, and Tevis decided on a sudden nap to avoid the pain. One would never want to suggest that a brave, gentleman and an officer had passed out. But the thing was out and the arrowhead hadn't detached in his leg. If it didn't infect, he'd probably live.

Tevis was quiet, sleeping. Now alone with nothing but Apaches to distract me, I had time to think. Why had I joined the Foreign Legion, the Arizona Rangers? Was I giving up on Alice Ann too easily? Where was my resolve? Didn't I love her beyond imagination and beyond all others? Yes, I thought I did, and she was in danger, not from Apaches, which I was fighting, but from white outlaws.

Outlaws, an interesting word. In England it meant men who had been stripped of their rights. Anyone was free to abuse and exploit them. They banded together for protection and to exploit others. They could be shot on sight, since they had no rights, but they were more a menace than before they'd lost them. They could not settle. They had to remain outside the law. Here it was not the same. These men chose to band together outside the law because the law was weak. They still had rights and were protected by the law that they abused. Most men think themselves good. Some find a wrong done themselves or their families and in breaking the law, seek to right the injustice, or so they claim. It is an excuse only, a way to think themselves good. The men I was dealing with, did not, I thought, think themselves good. They reveled in being bad without excuses.

The Helligans might think themselves righting a wrong by hunting me down for killing their kin, but I doubt even they really believed they had been wronged. They'd lost a man, and failure to avenge their leader's demise made them look weak. They couldn't have that. They wanted people to be terrified of them, and folks were cooperating with them by being terrified.

My cattle were gone. There didn't seem to be any point in starting a new herd. They might only steal it again. *Cappen* Ewell would never accept defeat. He'd taught me not to either. Was I accepting defeat or simply seeing reality?

Tevis groaned. My conscience had me in as much pain as he.

I still had the mine and my friends and Alice Ann, my *piskie* maiden, so young, lithe, and innocent, to protect.

A thought crossed my mind. Was I enthralled with the elfin lass because she represented my lost youth and safe harbor and home? Did her *fairie*-self remind me of Cornwall far away and years ago? Was I in love with a dream of home, hearth, and stary-gazy pie, of Cornish cooking with saffron and currants, mild and warm with coddled cream, and so unlike the local chili peppers? Of bread soft, warm and smelling of heaven instead of flat and chewy tortillas that had no odor until you added beans and chili? I put these thoughts aside.

What would *me* mother, a good Methodist, have me do? Why, a good Methodist would consult the scriptures and pray for an answer. Methodist, I might be, but I was no good Methodist and hadn't a Bible. I might pray to Saint Peran, fickle saint that he was. He'd help his friends, no matter the cost, and his help could be prodigious. Thrown into the Irish Sea by the wicked Irish with a millstone chained to his leg, he'd walked across the water all the way to Cornwall. Why, even Jesus hadn't had a millstone. I had a mine now, and he was the patron of miners. Perhaps he'd listen. I'd go back and rouse my friends. The odds were no worse than General Taylor faced at Buena Vista. Then I realized I'd prayed and got an answer. Perhaps I wasn't such a bad Methodist.

The clatter of shod hooves on stone brought me alert. I crawled to the entrance and looked up into the face of a mounted man.

"Can you boys use a hand?" asked Captain Jack.

Chapter 26 - A New Plan

I looked up at Swilling from my cave. "Good *ta* see *ya*, *Cappen*. I didn't hear any shooting. Did you happen to have taken any *o'* the heathen?"

He shook his head. "Not a one. We stayed low in the washes, but they're wary devils and saw us coming. How's the lieutenant?"

"Whilst I was carving the arrow from his leg, he suddenly decided to take a nap. He's sleeping like a babe, and I *'aven't* the *'eart* to wake *'im*. He'll be all right, I suppose, if it wasn't *pisonned*."

"Crawl out of there," said Swilling. "Your horse told us where to find you."

Cocking my head, I looked at him. Swilling was mad as a hatter and full of fun.

"He found the troop," the captain said, "and we followed his tracks back here until we heard shots."

"Well, that's it, then," I said. "I've got my kit, and I'll be going. Look after Lieutenant Tevis."

"But we're on campaign!" he stammered.

"Do we have an official status that you can compel me to stay?" He shook his head. "I thought not. I've just had a close call and accomplished nothing. It's time to return to my own affairs."

"It was a waste of the troop's time saving your useless butt!" he growled.

"If I'm useless, 'tis all the more reason I should go. *Cappen*, we're not accomplishing much. They're on watch for us. Those we catch in camp are probably not the ones causing trouble else they'd be watching for us."

Cappen Jack thought about this. "I know we make a late start after raids, but if they're driving stock, we take it from them and teach them a lesson. By catching them in their camps, we teach them to leave us alone."

"More often," I replied, "we stir them up. With the infantry among us at Fort Buchanan and the dragoons desperately far off at Fort Breckenridge, the Army isn't accomplishing much at all. Half their officers were gone; many went to their homes in the South and commissions at higher rank than they could have hoped in the U.S. Army. I'm going to stay closer to those I care for." Soon afterwards, I took my horse and bid my comrades farewell. During the ride to Casa Blanca, where else did I have to go? I formulated a plan.

"Don Hombre," said Juan Largo, my Apache Manso friend, "you are *muy loco*."

The Great Western, Sarah Bowman, shook her head sadly tossing her strawberry tresses. "I fear an injury from when they tossed you in the mine. Does your head still hurt?"

At *kindle teening* the Casa Blanca was crowded, noisy, full of smoke, and the smell of unwashed miners, field hands, and *vaqueros*. The girls giggled and led men off to private liaisons while others sat with men who were enjoying their first female company and decent meal in weeks or months. None of the Helligan gang, at least those we knew, was present.

"We face two threats: Pinal Apaches and Mexican banditos. Robinson and his Helligan friends want Alice Ann along with the Casa Blanca and the Boundary Hotel. They'll be back for these soon. . ."

"They've been quiet," said Sarah doubtfully.

"They'll be back," I replied firmly. "They won't forget the insult, and they know we've lost Ewell.

"They're playing a dangerous game," I continued. "They're trading guns to the Mexicans and to the Apaches who are using them to kill each other. If the two sides were to find out about this arrangement, both would turn on the Helligans."

"How do you make this happen?" asked Juan. "If you just ride in and tell them both, they will believe you and maybe let you live as a kindness. I would not go to Sonora, *jefe.* There they think every gringo is a land pirate, a filibuster."

"Nor," said red-headed Sarah, "should you go to the Pinal Apaches. They would suspend you from a tree, head down, and light a small fire to make sure your brains were fried."

"Aye," I responded, "but they respect the insane as touched by the gods." I grinned. "Which puts me in mind of needing Paddy Graydon and Ole Mose Carson for this chore."

Juan shook his head sadly. Great Western stood, saying, "I want no part of your suicide. If you're daft about Alice Ann, go see her, but don't ask me to take a hand helping you kill yourself."

The name alone made my head spin. I thought of her so graceful, slim, and beautiful, with long soft strawberry hair that smelled of saffron and currants. I became useless to the discussion, dreaming for her.

From outside there was a thunder of hooves loud enough to stop conversation and turn all heads toward the door. Jacko and Tallon Helligan filled the entryway followed closely by the Pellewes, Hellyar, and Turk.

"You there, Bowman," said Jacko, "sit with me. We've things to discuss."

Sarah rosc to her full height, tall as any man in the room, and standing her ground, said, "I've nothing to discuss with you." The ice in that statement gave me the chills. There was a fine *clacker* in that woman's head. She was the kind of woman a man should love, if only she were younger, more cultured, and gentle. She was a rough-bred, hill-county lass from Tennessee or Kentucky, even she wasn't sure, who'd followed the army for many years. She could curse like a dragoon sergeant and drink many of them under the table.

"Why, madam," said Jacko, "we have the division of profits between business partners to discuss. I've always wanted to own a whorehouse."

I was contemplating odds, and they weren't good. We couldn't count on backing from any of the customers. It was me, Sarah, and Juan against four powerful men. Any shooting would lead to many deaths, and we were outnumbered. It was *kicklish* that we might survive.

It was Tallon who opened the ball by grabbing Luz's hair and yanking her aloft from the lap of the miner she'd been courting. Luz screamed.

Then Guadalupe screamed, "*Hermanas, arriba a la carga!*"

And the Valkyries flew, each of the sisters to a man's back, claws extended, raking faces and eyes.

Turning to Sarah, I said, "You've trained them well I see."

"Idiot! *A la carga*!" she encouraged. "Charge!"

With rifle barrel, pistols, and fists we went to work *pasting* the foemen while the lasses attacked from the rear encumbering arms and blinding eyes. Fearsome the Valkyrie were that night. Thrown, hit, and bruised the señoritas always returned to the fray.

Luz kicked her way free striking some tender zones. I saw Guadalupe up on Turk's back raking his face deep as he bucked and turned. The girl did herself proud as any *vaquero* clinging to the bucking man and never losing her seat. Juan Largo bashed him in the face, and I saw blood spurt from his nose. Maria was on Jacko, and as he backed hard into the wall breaking her grip, I bashed him up the side of his head with my rifle.

"That's no way to treat a fine lady." I looked down at him as Maria relieved him of his pistols.

Sarah, the flame haired Great Western, flailed Tallon with fists alone while two of her girls worried him from behind. One bit off a chunk of his ear. Bleeding, he flung her to the ground. As he bent and drew back his huge fist to bash her head into the floor, she swallowed the ear for spite. I tried to get to her, but someone handed Sarah a rolling pin, and the fight soon went out of Tallon with a hand and arm broken and a knot on his head. The girls had disarmed him.

Hellyar stood no chance. Already encumbered by a lass, Sarah, Juan, and I hit him from all sides.

Soon we had the enemy disarmed and beaten to their knees. Turk lost an eye to Guadalupe's nail, which calmed him down considerable. In future, he'd wear an eye patch. It was quite the *capperause*. With the enemy in no condition to continue the affray, we escorted the foe to their horses and invited them to leave and never come back.

Sarah looked at me with blood dripping from a swollen lip. "Well, that tears it. We've no choice now. I'm in. Get Paddy and Mose and mount your campaign."

Juan Largo nodded his agreement.

Inside the Casa Blanca bruised and bloodied señoritas sang Spanish songs of victory. El Cid was mentioned and his wonderful horse, Juan Bautista de Anza; his victory over Cuerna Verde was lauded as was Santa Anna and his victory over the French. All that was missing was a Viking song about the Valkyrie. Then I recalled, the Valkyrie came to collect the souls of brave warriors who had died in battle. Not such a good omen. Heroes we might soon be and dead as well.

Chapter 27 - No Plan Survives Contact with the Enemy

Sitting against the adobe wall by the *zaguan*, the wagon gate, outside Robinson's in Tucson, Juan looked safe enough. The old man had spunk. The big sombrero hid his face and upper body, but he might still be recognized. He had to walk to and from his vantage point, and he or his limp might be recognized. The Helligans were just down the street. They might shoo him away, and when he stood my tall friend's face might be seen. He had *cajones*. Call him *manso*, but he was anything but tame. He was *bra* or, as the Mexicans say, a *bravo*.

Taking a *chanst* just being in town, I'd be of little help. They knew me and just being here in Tucson was *kicklish*. They knew my way of talking, and I had to be careful who I spoke to and how I spoke so as not to speak Cornish, which might be recognized. Wanting to be near enough to help Juan, I tried to move from place to place naturally and at the same time being close enough to help.

At the end of the first day of our watch, Juan came into our camp at the Rillito Wash north of town. The wash provided firewood and cover.

"Don Hombre," he confided, "it is hard to believe. They talk in front of me. They think I am a *tonto*, a deaf mute, sleeping Mexican who cannot understand them, who is like the adobe wall."

I waited. Unable to stand it any longer, I asked, "So what did they say?"

"They talked about their contacts in Santa Cruz, Rodolfo Rodriquez and his *tenente*, Hernan Sanchez."

"Yes, we knew that Juan."

Juan smiled. He was having too much fun dragging this out. "They talked about where they meet and even gave their sign and countersign. And I heard they meet Cuchillo Colorado of the Pinal Apaches on the north slope of the Owl Head Buttes."

"Owl Head Buttes? I don't know them."

Juan nodded. "I do. They are a day's ride northwest of here."

I was stunned. "They said all this in front of you? They are *wiffleheads*." A thought struck me, and I went on. "The only road that goes anything close to north is the Butterfield Mail road . . ."

He cut me off. "They won't use that. They will go by Canada del Oro so those who see them may think them prospectors, which will explain the large packs on their mules."

"We must pick a place of ambush," I said, "and I will go and get Paddy and Mose. When do they take rifles to the Pinal?"

"I do not know," said Juan. "Perhaps they will say *maña*."

A thousand questions occurred to me. Chief among them was to question where they were getting the rifles."

"From San Diego, I think," said Juan answering the unasked question. "They use the *Jornada del Diablo*, the Devil's Highway, across the low desert to Yuma."

The Butterfield Road, which connected the nation from St. Louis to San Francisco by way of Fort Smith, Arkansas, Tucson. and Los Angeles, followed the Gila River far to the north. The *Jornada* went from *tinaja* to *tinaja*, rock tanks that held a little water after the rains. They were hard to find and might be empty when found. It was not a busy road, but anyone who knew it could cross the desert.

Juan continued his vigil day after day. Mose and Paddy joined us in the campsite, waiting for our next move. Finally, after days, Juan heard what we had waited for. The guns had arrived, and they would take twenty of them north that night to Owl Head Buttes. We rode hard to arrive at our chosen ambush ahead of them.

A good ambush depends on surprise. *Cappen* Ewell had taught me that surprise was not the same as startling someone. Surprise is presenting the enemy with a situation to which they have no viable response. Unfortunately, not every enemy is intelligent enough to know he's been surprised. We picked a site where the canyon walls were too steep with overhanging rocks to allow escape to the sides, so the enemy must retreat or charge through. We then blocked the narrow canyon floor at a spot where they would not see the obstruction until they came around a bend and were on top of it.

Juan and Mose took positions behind the rocks where, when they emerged, they'd be looking down on the pack train from above and behind.

"I'll step into their path," I told the others, "and demand that they dismount and disarm." Flour sacks with eyeholes would conceal our features. We intended to take them alive and leave them on foot.

"Aye, that ought to work," said Paddy, who would be beside me, scowling, his sombrero pulled low over his eyes, his poncho concealing him.

We heard them coming far off, and Juan from his higher vantage told us there were four riders and two pack mules. Slithering down deeper into the shadows, we waited.

"*Halto mi amigos!*" I dcmanded in my best Mexican, stepping hooded from cover in poncho and sombrero when they were 10 yards off. In the moonlight, the clicks of my weapon coming to full cock sounded loud. I leveled my rifle at Hellyar Pellewe's heart. Turk must be back in Tucson nursing the socket where his eye had been.

Hellyar squirmed and made his decision. Spurring his horse, he tried to draw his pistol as he charged. My rifle boomed and shot flame. Hellyar fell, his heart poisoned by a ball of lead. Rifles cracked above me, and pistols joined the affray. A horse reared and fell on its rider who, game to the end, continued to fire his pistol until a bullet silenced him. Beside me, a horse knocked Paddy to the ground. I turned to fire on the escaping rider, and then saw him trapped and dragging on the ground a boot stuck in a stirrup.

A horse galloped back the way the riders had come, a rider low on his back.

"I'm sure I hitted 'im!" called Mose. "Kilt him sure." Maybe. Strange things can happen between dying men and horses.

Though time seemed to stretch forever, the fight was over in seconds, and two men lay dead at our feet.

It took us an hour to gather in the pack animals and remaining horse. We even found the one that had dragged its rider to death and freed the animal of his gory burden.

"What do we do now?" asked Paddy.

We had planned to leave the Helligan men afoot and head back toward Tucson skirting the town along

Rillito Wash. But with one man possibly ahead of us, this wasn't a good idea.

"We skirt the Santa Catalinas on the north side," I said, "and head for the San Pedro River."

Paddy stammered. "But that's all Pinal Apache country, and the Injuns are waiting for these guns."

I considered for a moment the lurking Apache awaiting a shipment of guns. "They're waiting at Owl Head Buttes northwest of here. We're headed the other way, southeast. Hopefully, most of the Pinals will be at Owl Heads. It'll be light soon. We'd better get moving." I paused. "I wonder who the Helligans will think was responsible."

Mose spoke up. "If'n that rider don't make it ta home, me'be they'll think it was Injuns."

Maybe. Or their Mexican *amigos*. After all, who else knew about their illegal transactions?

I whispered a prayer of thanks to Jesus and Saint Peran and asked them to keep protecting us. My Methodist upbringing said it was wrong to prayer to Saint Peran, but any saint who liked beer and walked across the sea with a millstone bound to his leg was someone I wanted on my side. I'd fashion a flag of black with a white cross, I thought, and fly it from a Mexican roadside shrine. That should please the saint, his colors and symbol. *Me* mother had tried to guide me, but I'd become a smuggler and a rogue. I wasn't sure Methodism could save me.

We rode through the rest of the night, stopped for breakfast, and rested our horses and ourselves. Any pursuit would be far behind unless Pinals had spotted us. Even so, they'd have miles of catching up to do. The San Pedro Valley as far south as the Butterfield Road was their raiding ground, and travelers disappeared frequently. Apaches didn't attack Butterfield's stages; they carried little but the mail and nothing the Apache wanted. Moreover, Butterfield's people gave them supplies. Most of the immigrant trains going down the San Pedro on Leach's Wagon Road (north, the way the river runs) were too large and heavily armed to interest the Indians. But people alone and small groups disappeared all the time, vanishing without notice.

Long stretches of the San Pedro were dry above Butterfield's San Pedro Station. Leach's Wagon Road was avoided for lack of water and because folks who hadn't seen a town in over 300 miles were willing to stop for supplies in any town, even Tucson. As we went south along Southern Immigrant Trail built by the Mormon Battalion where it followed the river above San Pedro, we passed a train of eight wagons. That was pretty typical. The Chiricahua Apache weren't yet raiding Americans. They were accepting gifts from Butterfield and the Indian agent and raiding down into Sonora. That would change when the governor of the Mexican state decided to offer better gifts.

Eight wagons were small enough not to put strain on resources of water and grass and large enough to discourage most raiders. I saw that the wagons were nearly empty. They started out with supplies for trail packed to the canvas. There was no room for beds, pianos, or grandfather clocks. Just supplies. And by the time they'd come this far, the food was nearly gone.

Chapter 28 - A New Threat

We turned up the Babocomari River and before long spied an approaching dust cloud.

Mose Carson stared long and hard into the dust. "I think it's friends, but we best make ourselves scarce until we knows fer sure."

Out of the dust emerged a column of marching men lead by a bearded lieutenant mounted on a mule. Despite the bushy beard, he looked little more than a child. The hat he wore, blue with a brass hunting horn device, rose six and half inches above the brim tapering in slightly. The left side brim was folded up. Device and the fold of the brim indicated that he was infantry. Two dozen or so of his men rode mules, the others, nearly forty more, marched behind, and in the rear pack mules were led. This was an army on campaign and as large a force as had been fielded in this region since the Mexican War.

I recognized Johnny Ward, a rancher, and emerging from concealment hailed him. "Johnny, what's up?"

"Apaches, Bray, Chiricahuas. They've taken my boy and my cattle."

"Chiricahuas?" I replied. "I thought they were at peace."

"Sir," said the infantry leader, "I am Lieutenant Bascom, 7th Infantry. We are in pursuit of the raiders. Their trail follows this river and points toward Apache Pass. That is the home of Cochise. I am directed to go there and get the boy and have the cattle returned. There will be no war unless Cochise chooses to make one."

I responded, "Well, *cappen*, looks like you've got the force to make it happen."

Paddy called out, "I can't miss this. I'm going with the wee lad."

Mose, Juan, and I continued on to the rancho where we gathered wood to light the hearth and attract our Chiricahua trading partners.

Striking a Lucifer, I was about to torch the kindling, but instead I withdrew my hand and blew out the flame. "I can't do it. It ain't right."

Juan spoke first. "You've sold guns to *Indios* before."

"Those were for hunting. I never had a mind to ask them to raid folks afore."

"But," said Mose, "they're Mezikans and *bandidos* who wants the guns to raid our friends."

"Not all," I said. "Some are just *peones* at the mercy of every man with a gun."

"Bravo, Don Hombre. We will not sell the guns to the Apache."

Pulling out my nose-warmer, I packed it with *bacca* and brought it alight, thinking as I did so. "We'll take the guns to Casa Blanca. They'll make us stronger, and we'll steal a shipment headed for Santa Cruz. Maybe it will be enough to make the Apaches and the Mexican bandidos suspicious of each other and especially of the Helligans."

We'd first learned of the guns Palatine Robinson and the Helligans were selling to Mexicans and Pinal Apaches from Robinson's wife when we rescued Alice Ann, my *piskie* maid who would no longer speak to me. Only when we opened the packs did we learn that these were Sharps breech-loading percussion rifles. The Army was using muzzle loading muskets that were less accurate than rifles, though soldiers could get off three rounds per minute with them. Many civilians had rifles accurate to twice the range, 200 or 300 yards, but which took almost a minute to reload because the ball had to be forced through the rifling down the long barrel. The Sharps took a paper cartridge like the Army used. Drop the breech, push in the cartridge, add a cap and you were loaded. The charge pushed the ball through the rifling for you. Even a slow man could get off six rounds a minute, and the Sharps had the range and accuracy of a rifle. One of the reasons Apaches didn't attack Butterfield Stations was because Butterfield had had the foresight to arm his men with Sharps. Short of canon, they were the deadliest weapons available to anyone.

Back at the Casa Blanca, Juan, Moses, and Great Western gathered with me at the table.

"Sharps!" Mose yelped.

I sucked on *mi* nose-warmer and blew a bit of a smoke ring. "And the truly devilish thing is that their customers would be dependent on Robinson and the Helligans for cartridges. *Tantarabobus* his own self *couldna* done better."

"Maybe not," said Great Western. "Cartridges are no great trick to make. The Army will be leaving soon. They're going back to the Rio Grande to defend us from the Texians and leaving us here to defend ourselves from Apaches armed with Sharps rifles."

"And from Mexicans," said Juan without explanation.

"He's right," I said. "When the Sonorans hear that the army is gone and the country splitting up, they're sure to try to grab a piece for themselves. We done the same to them."

"Saints preserve us," moaned Paddy who had just entered returning from 16 days at Apache Pass with Lieutenant Bascom. "And we squabble with the Helligans. Things did not go well at the Pass. Cochise is upset, and so in Mangas Coloradas and Francisco of the Coyotero."

Great Western frowned. "No more of that. We have no choice. Like it or not, we have three enemies and no one but ourselves to defend our stake."

"Then," I replied, "we have to raid them again. Get Sharps for ourselves and maybe make them suspicious of each other."

"Guadalupe will go as our spy to Tucson," said the Amazon.

I looked at Great Western without comprehension. "It's too dangerous."

"It's too dangerous," she said, "for Juan to go again. She has a stake in the coming conflict, and she wants to help."

I didn't like sending a woman in harm's way, but arguing with Sarah Bowman, the Great Western, is like spitting into the wind.

"Go see your girlfriend before it's too late," she ordered.

The next day I escorted Guadalupe to Tucson. We stopped by Alice Ann's rancho.

Alice was elated. "Lupe, I'm so glad to see you! There just aren't any young women around to talk to."

I smiled at Alice Ann, my *piskie* maiden. "I'm escorting Guadalupe to Tucson to buy some new clothes."

Alice turned away from me to face Lupe. "So, Lupe," she asked, "why have you come visiting me?" The lass completely ignored my presence and everything I said.

Alice Ann made us a picnic lunch, which we took down by the waters of Sonoita Creek under a giant cottonwood. She wouldn't speak to me. She and Lupe, the maiden and the harlot, prattled happily while combing and plaiting each other's hair. I was excluded but overheard their words.

"Palatine came by to see me," said Alice. "He says he'll come and take me away soon and marry me. He can't come as often as he'd like. Father is angry with him over something, and Palatine has to avoid him."

Her words were not welcome news. We'd tried to tell her that Palatine Robinson was married to Elvira whom many held to be the most beautiful woman in Arizona. I tried to explain he planned to sell her to a Mexican bordello, but she didn't believe that Robinson was a low down cheat and liar with evil intentions for her. She was still in love with him.

Riding on toward Tucson, Lupe tried to console me. "Bray, she is *muy bonita* and a good girl, an innocent. She does not understand evil men like *Señor* Robinson."

My heart was heavy again. My true love was rejecting me, and she was making it difficult to protect her. Even her father realized there was a problem, but the child wouldn't listen. I prayed to Jesus and Saint Peran for her protection, but prayer didn't lift my spirits. I was haunted, wondering if I could stay married to a woman so foolish. She was just a girl, young and innocent.

Lupe floated through Helligan society, invisible as a human being, a mere object. She was Mexican of no consequence and not worth notice. Men spoke in front of her, not realizing she could speak English. They ignored her presence, except to use her as a woman. She was an appliance, a bit of furniture, and she brought back marvelous amount information. Staying close to Lupe, I listened in saloons, keeping my hat low over my eyes and being careful to keep the Cornish out of my language.

The Bucket 'O Blood stank of spilled whiskey and *pulque*, vomit, tobacco, spit, and worse. The low ceiling blackened by smoke hovered low over the heads of those standing at the bar, a plank set between barrels. The adobe room was tiny; barely room for the bar and a few tables. I sat hunched over my drink in the darkest corner. Unable to stand the choking stench a second longer, I slid out into the night air, leaving Lupe smiling sweetly and leaning on Tallon Helligan's arm.

Even beyond the adobe walls I could hear a woman's shriek and the thumping of fists on human flesh, followed by coarse laughter. Lupe slid out the door on her face; she was bleeding. I knelt beside her.

"It's okay, Bray. We can go. I know when they go to Santa Cruz with guns."

I looked at her poor beaten and bloodied face and without thought or a word ran back into the saloon and commenced the *capperause* by striking Tallon in the ear as hard as I could. He shook it off, towering over me with great ox-like shoulders. I'd struck the wrong part. His brain was already damaged and more damage there was of little use. I dodged a huge fist, devastating but slow, managing my own strikes that seemed not to inflict much pain. He tried a bear hug but I eluded him. He swung again and connected with my jaw. I heard church bells but managed to remain conscious as the floor came up to greet me.

As I lay there, Tallon drew his pistol. In the click of his weapon being cocked, I heard Death coming for me. A woman screamed, Lupe. Tallon looked up. I drew and shot him in the throat. One of his companions reached for his gun as I scrambled to my feet. Mine was already out, and I shot him in the belly. Lupe pulled me through the door into the dark night.

"We must run!" she yelled as I halted putting two shots into the door to discourage pursuit.

The Helligan gang had a core of trust, their relatives. Now Tallon was gone and Hellyar, too. Turk was wearing an eye patch. Robinson was in the next circle of trust, smooth, educated, and perhaps possessing some honor. O'Malley, who posed as Bontrager, was lying low but was probably in the same circle of trust as Robinson, though a potential rival. Jacko Helligan, smart though he was, no longer had leaders he could trust. There were still plenty of outlaws to choose from, but he couldn't really trust them. They were outlaws, men who knew no law except themselves, men who only thought of themselves. They were liars and cheats and some of them cowards. He could only keep them in line through fear, and he bad luck that weakened his hold. He'd lost a shipment of Sharps rifles, and the Apache were upset at promises broken.

No one was afraid of Robinson, though they should have been. A coward, he would happily shoot an enemy in the back. They feared O'Malley after what he'd done to Brunckow. He might try to take over again. Jacko had problems. There really isn't any honor among thieves.

Chapter 29 - Viva Mexico

A few well-placed shots at the door of the Bucket 'O Blood delayed pursuit long enough for Lupe to get our horses saddled. Once out of town and hidden by an inky night, we were safe. No one would follow before dawn. We would be long gone by then and back among friends.

"We can't dress up as Apaches!" roared Paddy Graydon rising from his seat at the Casa Blanca.

"Yes, we can," I replied. "A little walnut juice to darken our skin, we keep our distance and let only Juan be seen up close."

Not happy at all, Paddy mumbled something as he sat. I continued, saying, "Getting out of Tucson in the dark of the night and disappearing into the wilds, it was an easy thing for their trading ventures to go unnoticed." The others, Juan, Paddy, Old Mose, and Sarah, nodded. "But going to Santa Cruz, they have to pass down the populated valley. The road goes through Tubac. It will take them two or three days on an established road. There are only a few places they can stop where there is water. They must look like others carrying goods to Sonora. Too many guards will give them away."

"So?" demanded Paddy.

"We pick them up at Tubac," I replied, "and hit them where they stop for the night."

Moses Carson grunted. "'Paches don't like to fight at night. Skeert of evil spirits. Me'be we could dress as Mezicans agin."

I shook my head. "We want them suspicious of both their trading partners and their partners suspicious of them in turn." I went on, "Juan will watch for them in Tubac.

Depending how they're traveling and the time of day they pass, there'll only be a few places they can stop for the night." I wasn't so sure that watering places were limited to just a few easy to locate spots, but I did my best to sound confident.

Four days later, when the sun was just past its zenith, Juan crossed the Santa Cruz River to join us in the hills. "Oh, Don Hombre, you cannot believe our luck." I waited knowing he wanted me to ask. Finally, "There are only three. One walks beside a *carreta* pulled by an ox. He and one of the others are *Mexicanos*. Two ride. One is the trader, O'Malley."

Mose grinned. "They'll stop at Guevavi where thar's a spring. Won't make it a step past." He tested the draw on his bow. "Hain't used one in yars." The grin got bigger.

"We'll head there now and hide," I said. "Approach during the night. Strike at dawn."

We were able to observe the slow crawl of their dust from miles back in the hills and watched as they camped for the night. Leaving the horses behind, we approached afoot dressed as Apaches. They were careless of their watch, thinking themselves close enough to settlements to be safe, I suppose.

In the dawn's gray twilight, we approached their *carreta* and horses. A horse whinnied and stamped, awakening their sleeping guard. As he started to cry out, Juan put an arrow through his throat. Roused, the others reached for their weapons. Mose charged bow in hand, giving a chilling war hoop. He put an arrow into one of the Mexicans and Juan, limping along behind, joined it with a second.

O'Malley, confronted by a giant 'Pache, ran for his life, cracking off a few wild shots at his assailants. Mose loved a good ruckus, and Juan soon got in the spirit, stumping along as fast as he could.

Paddy and I unpacked the wagon and secured the cases to the horses' backs, leaving the ox and *carreta* behind. I fired a shot when we were loaded to alert our friends and headed off toward the spot where we'd left our horses. Juan and Mose soon joined us happy as kids.

"Put a arrow tru' O'Malley's leg," laughed Mose. "Juan's a good a shot as me."

Juan grinned. "Señor O'Malley take long time walk to Tubac."

Back at the Casa Blanca, we heard rumors. The Helligans were having trouble with their trading partners. Shipments had been paid for and not delivered. There was suspicion.

"This is crazy," insisted our wise friend, Sarah Bowman, as she helped us pack two mules with goods including two Sharps rifles.

I nodded. "Needs to be done."

Juan, Paddy, always game for a crazy scheme, and me set off for Santa Cruz in Sonora. Arriving there, we sought the hacienda of Rodolfo Rodriguez.

Juan said nothing, but Paddy whistled. "You think he has enough guards? I can see six."

Bold as brass, we rode right up to the guards at the gate. There we unpacked the two Sharps rifles. The guards unceremoniously disarmed us and rudely ushered us in to see the don.

"Don Rodolfo," I began, "Señor Palatine Robison sends these in token of good faith."

Rodolfo glared. "How are these good faith? I have already paid for 20, and even these are late in coming."

I did my best to sweat. It wasn't hard. Even money said he'd kill us. "Señor Robinson is having difficulty with supplies."

He bought the story concerning supply problems. Everyone had supply problems. Apaches and banditos and the long, hot, lonely desert made sure of that. We sold him the remaining goods at heavily discounted prices. They even returned our weapons. Sure that we'd be followed, the three of us repaired to a cantina for drinks. The Mexican cantina was an adobe that had seen better days and smelled better in its youth. There were no tables or chairs, just a banco around three walls and a plank for a bar. Tequila and pulque were available. The locals stared at us, coldly hostile, but not doing anything about their hatred of the gringos drinking among them. We were armed, and they were not, at least, not until Don Rodolfo's men entered. We spilled quite a bit and gave the impression that we'd consumed more than we ought. We were after all lawless men, and our boss was far away in Tucson. We could drink up some of his money from the trade, and who would know?

Whispering to Paddy, sure that I'd be overheard and my indiscretion reported, I said, "The old fool bought it."

"Aye, laddie," he replied, "there are other buyers paying higher prices."

Back and forth we went, with minor indiscretions repeated occasionally for Juan's "benefit" in Spanish just in case there were no English speakers among the eavesdroppers. Then we headed for our horses, but found ourselves unexpectedly pursued.

"Fire on 'em!" yelled Paddy and I did but in turning to fire, I fell and became a prisoner.

The next morning, Don Rodolfo, was not about to rouse himself in the late evening, I found myself tied to a post in the don's courtyard. The whip bit through my shirt and tore into my flesh. I bled from a score of wounds. Tied to a post, I could only cringe and cry out. "Don Rodolfo, I'll tell you anything you want to know!"

"Who has my rifles?"

"Yes, yes," I said pleading for my life, "he sold them to Pinal Apaches. He got a better price. There will be more, I promise." The whip bit me again.

The don gestured to two of his men. "Take this garbage out and dispose of it away from my hacienda."

"Wait, Don, no," I pleaded. "If you kill me, Robinson will not trust you."

He considered how the killing might affect his relations with Robinson. "I think not. I will send him a message to deliver on time and in full by disposing of you."

It's difficult to be sanguine when you're bleeding, so I tried to tell myself, "Oh well, that didn't work." Nearly unconscious and in pain, there was little else I could do but think Don Rodolfo an ungrateful sod and wish the devil take him. I threw in a prayer to Saint Peran. Might as well pray, I thought, even if it hadn't worked before. Two men cut me down and hauled me across the courtyard and into the molded darkness of the covered entry to the zaguan, the big gate. They had to expend most of their effort dragging me. I'm a big man, and I didn't feel much like walking. Perhaps I should have been noble and brave and marched out walking upright with my torn back bleeding and my head high. I could have put on a right show and made a speech: "I'm sorry I have but one life to give for my *bandito jefe*." But, I really didn't feel like it. I felt more like being a pain in the butt, so they had to drag me, and the two were bent double with the effort.

As we emerged from the darkened, covered entry, Juan slit the belly of one of the encumbered men and then his throat. As the other reached for his gun, Paddy cracked him on the head so hard it left a bloodied dent. The vaquero wouldn't be waking up again in this lifetime.

"Can you make it?" asked Paddy. I nodded yes, and we ran for the horses. It's amazing how life returns to the near dead when you're properly motivated. I wasn't all that badly injured anyway.

Mounted and well away from the hacienda, Paddy asked, "Did it work?"

"I think so. Don Rodolfo is not happy with Robinson or the Pinal."

Paddy pulled out a medal that hung about his neck. "God bless St. Patrick, patron of Ireland and lost causes."

I didn't have a medal handy but I called out, "And God bless Saint Peran!"

We disappeared into rugged hill country where we'd be hard to track. The border country offers many possibilities for going unseen.

Chapter 30 - The Civil War

"I can't run a mine without mail service!" protested Sylvester Mowry owner of the Patagonia Mine and erstwhile Army officer banging his fist on the table. Heads turned throughout the sala of the Casa Blanca. "Better we should join the Confederacy than be left to rot on the vine."

Charles Poston glared at him. "Keep your voice down, Sly. Talk like that won't get us made a territory."

Paddy Graydon snorted. "The Butterfield Overland Mail packed up in March at Congress's insistence and left us high and dry. Rumors say the Army will be headed back East soon to fight a war with the Confederacy. The Confederacy wants us, even in the Union don't. They'll send men to protect us, and they'll get the mail running again."

"Yes," said Poston, "they sent J.J. Giddings to reopen the southern road in April for the San Antonio and San Diego Mail, the Jackass Mail. And look how well that turned out."

At Doubtful Canyon, Cochise and his warriors stopped J.J. Giddings and four companions, traveling in a borrowed Overland celerity wagon. The Apaches had hung the men head down from trees over a small pile of ash. Many of the Butterfield men and much of the stock was still out there at the stations waiting and hoping someone would reopen the mail route.

"Lots of officers have left already," added Great Western. "They been offered commissions at higher rank by their home states and the recognition they've long deserved. You can't blame them."

"Cochise," I said, "has latched on to a *capperause* since the Butterfield packed it in. At least 10 men lie dead at Doubtful Canyon, and more have disappeared near San Simon."

Poston turned pale. "We can't survive without the Army."

"Get used to it, Chucky." Only Sly would address Poston thus. Mr. Poston preferred Charles or Mister or Mister Poston or Don Carlos or Master of All He Surveys. Sly, on the other hand, while on Army assignment in Utah had seduced Brigham Young's pretty daughter-in-law. The Army got him out of the Kingdom of Deseret under cover of darkness, but he seemed to have left his career behind. Sly Mowry was careless that way.

Chucky remained pale. "What do we do if the Army leaves?"

Paddy shrugged. "Then we leave, too."

Luz, prettiest of Sarah's girls, walked to our table and then sat on Mowry's lap. "There's my cue," he said cheerfully, arising with the girl in his arms and heading for the stairs.

Sarah, the Great Western, frowned and looked at the table top. "I'm afraid Paddy's right. Most of my business comes from the army and the mines. The farmers and stockmen won't stay with no one to feed. If the Army goes, I leave."

The light was dim in the windowless adobe building. A few smoky lanterns lighted the room. The fine smell of dinner lingered in the close air but was slowly being replaced by the smell of *bacca* and spilled tequila. Smoke misted the air as a few vaqueros and miners drank, gambled, and paid court to Sarah's girls. It was a typical evening, except for the lack of soldiers from Fort Buchanan.

The door opened and Jacko Helligan and Seamus O'Malley, known locally as Dave Bontrager, murderer of Brunckow and his crew, crowded the entry. Jacko bore a Sharps and stood scanning, looking for someone. I sensed he had brought a crew now standing behind him in the dark.

Spotting Sarah, her red hair a standout, he called out, "Time's up, witch! We're takin' over."

I lurched from my chair, drew my big Dragoon Colt, and fired. He hadn't expected that and jumped away from the muzzle flame back out the door. My shot struck Seamus in the gut and drove him backward screaming.

Running toward the door, I fired to discourage them from trying to enter. "Bar the doors!" Ana barred the front door. I fired through it to discourage those beyond.

Paddy ran through the kitchen to the backdoor. I heard shots from his direction. Sarah's girls arose from chairs and laps and ran to get their new Sharps rifles. From above, I heard a boom followed by screaming from without the front door. "Good," I thought. "One of the girls is working the murder holes Sarah had made above the *portal,* the front entry hall.

Poston crawled across the floor. "Let me out! This isn't my fight!"

Chucky wasn't a coward. No man in Arizona in those days was nor could be. He had a keen notion of his own self-interest and an exaggerated sense of his importance.

"Sorry, Charles. No can do. They'd shoot you as you went out anyway."

He hugged the floor. Miners and vaqueros huddled in the corners seeking the safety of good adobe walls that absorbed bullets.

Sly skipped down the stairs, his long shirt the only covering to his modesty. "Give me a gun!"

From above, I could hear Sarah organizing the girls and Juan Largo. Soon, they started up a steady, rhythmic firing.

Concerned that Paddy hadn't returned from the back door, I called out, "Paddy, are you all right?"

"Fine, boyo, fine. I can't see anything but the door, but I'm fine."

Funny thing about outlaws, they like getting killed a good deal less than soldiers and men defending their property. The job only pays off if you survive, so heroism for outlaws is a low priority. Once they've lost the advantage, they are apt to seek the better part of valor.

"Paddy," I called, "if we can hold out till dawn, I think fire from the roof will drive them away."

My guess proved wrong. Under the cover of dark, one of Jacko's crew crawled right up to the kitchen door with oil and a torch concealed in an *olla*, a trick as old as Gideon in the Bible. All that was lacking was trumpets. Two shots rang out from the murder holes above the *portal* and a man screamed, wounded, and unable to move as the fire he had started flared up around him.

I ran to the kitchen door passing Paddy horrified at the thought of a man burning alive, even this one. "We've got to help him!"

"Let him burn." Paddy didn't move.

I pulled the door open to drag the man inside away from the fire. Shots came from the dark but missed me. The outlaw continued to burn, and I reached through flame to drag him in burning my hands in the process. The man was dead before I could beat out the flames. The fire still burned, and the door was still open.

Recognizing a new danger, I called out. "We've got to put it out! The door will light the *vigas* and the floor above."

Two miners ran to the door with a bucket of water and a pot of stew left from diner.

"No!" I yelled, "it'll spread the oil and the fire!" But too late, the liquid flew.

It didn't douse the fire. Rather it spread it, and in spreading it made it less intense near the door. I slammed it shut as the last of the fuel expended itself on impervious adobe walls.

Paddy sat grinning. "If they try that again, laddie, we may have a wee problem."

I turned to look at him in question.

"We're out of stew."

They didn't try it again. No one else, it seemed, was willing to risk the flames. Great Western made free with *tequila* and *arquardiente* among our unintended guests though we of the watch remained sober.

As the sun rose, our lookouts indicated that they could see nothing of the outlaws. Miners, *vaqueros,* and *charros* began to stagger out. No one impeded them.

"Great party, Western." Sly searched for his trousers. He'd apparently had a busy night.

From above, Luz, standing watch, called out, "Smoke! The fort, he burns!"

We joined her on the roof. The smoke was coming from the direction of Fort Buchanan though we couldn't see what was burning.

Sly looked stunned. "The outlaws have attacked the fort with fire?"

Paddy shook his head. "Dinna be daft, boyo. 'Tis the Army's way of departing, and I'll be going now."

Chapter 31 - Tubac, A Great Place to Raise Kids

Below us on a triangle of land where streams joined below the hills, Fort Buchanan burned fitfully.

Grundy Ake was indignant. “Army’s abandoning us. Least you could do is let us have the supplies ‘stead o’ burnin’ ‘em.”

“Orders,” replied Lieutenant Colonel Pitcairn Morrison, 7th Infantry, and lately commander of Fort Buchanan. He may have had orders, but I noticed that the fires hadn’t been well set and would soon go out on their own.

William Wordsworth spat. “You could have left it to the militia.” The provisional governor of Arizona had appointed him a major general of militia. Neither title had any standing in Washington or with the Army.

The colonel rode down the hill to take his place at the head of the column leaving the fort. At its rear, Paddy Graydon waved from the wagon he drove, taking with him what he could salvage from the Boundary Hotel. He’d arrived with no more than the uniform on his back, and now a civilian he knew how to make a living around soldiers.

“What do we do now?” Grundy asked of the wind.

The general replied. “We put out the fires, salvage what we can, and move ourselves to Tubac.”

Abner Crumpton stood there, mouth agape. “You mean I should give up my farm? All I own? I can’t do that.”

“Don’t see much choice,” said the general. “Apaches have already taken Johnny Ward’s boy. With the army gone, we’re wide open. And Cochise is riled up.

We'll start south, and each family can join as we pass. The stage road to Tubac will be a real fight."

Grundy nodded. "I don't see any other way. We could go south around the mountains to the Santa Cruz River, miles out of our way, and we'd still have to cross plenty of deep arroyos and stream beds."

Thus it was decided, all the Sonoita Creek settlers, except cantankerous Sly Mowry who would remain at his mine, would depart for safer circumstances.

Sarah Bowman, Juan, and I hid the *platino* near the Casa Blanca.

The tall redhead looked on our work. "We've trusted each other with our lives. I guess we'll have to trust each other now with our wealth."

I looked from one to the other of my friends. "There's no place near enough to exchange it for money."

Juan Largo commented sagely, "The *platino*, he likes the earth and will wait peacefully for us."

Sarah looked me in the eyes and then did the same with Juan. "I've got to stay with my girls, but you two can ride together. When the time comes, come and get me. I'm not hard to find."

Sic transit gloria. Thus glory passes or, in my case, glory and wealth. My cattle were stolen, my trading with Indians didn't work out because I couldn't bring myself to give them Sharps rifles, and my wealth from mining was back in the ground. I was pretty much reduced to what I'd arrived here with, the clothes on my back and my weapons. This wasn't entirely so. I had a few hundred in my pockets from the gold we'd mined. It wasn't the vast wealth and position that I'd almost had, but it would have to do. I also had a new friend, Juan.

I almost had a *fairie* princess, but reduced to poverty as I was, I didn't think she'd want me. She still thought me an uncultured beast. I'd had almost enough high-handedness from an unlettered, innocent farm girl with red hair, almost enough. It was she who was taken with a man in a slick suit, a gambler, liar, and cheat.

One by one, the families and wagons joined the train as it plodded southwest following the Sonoita Creek to the hot, lowlands along the Santa Cruz River and then turned west across the southern end of the Santa Rita Mountains towards Tubac where they might find security in numbers packed into a small adobe village. It was August, and the rains came daily, flooding dry streambeds and raising a torrent in the creek and river. The passage was slow and difficult, and the bottoms were quagmires full of mosquitos that left men sick.

The Crumptons joined. Abner gave up his farm after all. Alice Ann seemed to add the loss of her father's farm to my list of sins. She wouldn't look at me.

The wagons weren't heavily loaded. Wagons were for carrying food and trail supplies. Very little else was taken. Few folks had much to bring. At the first hard upward grade, we had to hitch six teams to the lead wagon to get it up the slope, which was followed rapidly by a hill going steeply down into the next arroyo. We hitched on chains and held the wagon back as it descended. Nonetheless, lowering the wagons down steep slopes was hair-raising and dangerous. It took all day to get the nine wagons across for a gain of less than a mile. The next day looked to be the same. Five days later, we came around a curve, and there before us was the river plain.

Nearing Tubac, I rode ahead as scout and was first to enter town. It was only luck that I spotted Jacko Helligan and his cousin, Turk Pellew, before they saw me. I counted six of their men on horseback guarding a wagon with a tightly drawn cover.

Turk pointed at me his one good eye glaring. "It's him, the one that killed your brother, Bane, in Santa Fe!"

I drew and fired without conscious thought. Without taking time to see if the shot went true, I jerked the reins and headed off the street behind a store where I climbed to stand on my horse's saddle and leapt to the low roof. Parapets might give some advantage, and until they figured out where I'd gone, they provided a concealed route to move about the flat-roofed town. I had only my knife and two Dragoon Colts plus powder, ball, and caps. Eleven shots, I figured, for there wouldn't be time to reload.

Below me, I could hear Jacko bellowing orders. I ran to the far end of the village, jumping between houses where there were gaps. Looking back, I saw hands appear on the parapet where I'd climbed up. A face followed, and I placed a bullet in it. Ten shots left and only seven outlaws still were standing.

I leapt to the ground near Poston's house and the old Presidio and ran uphill to get to the far side of the street.

"There he is!" Shots rang out and bullets danced around me. I tucked and rolled and rising fired a wild shot to discourage them.

"Get him!" Jacko roared as I ran behind the Presidio, the highest point in town. It was of some advantage. I caught glimpses of Jacko's men. Most were coming up the main street.

A man appeared gun in hand at the far end of the Presidio. I fired instinctively and hit him hard. He went down dropping his gun, and then still game, he tried to crawl to the mislaid weapon. I seized the pistol and shoved it into my belt. A shot grazed my thigh and spun me around. I managed to fall between buildings. It had come from the head of the main street near Poston's house. Their blood was up, and the conflict wouldn't be over until I killed Jacko or he killed me. Picking myself up, I limped between buildings and crossed the street.

Jacko roared, "There he is! Get him!"

He was still down at the low end of the main street near where I'd ascended the roof. You might think he'd want to confront me mano-a-mano and end this thing. No such luck. He was keeping to the rear. Where was Turk? I'd soon be surrounded, but I was between the gang and Jacko. It was time to go after him.

I charged down the middle of the street, limping as fast as I could, with both Dragoon Colts drawn and blazing. A bullet struck the heel of my boot and spun me off my feet knocking me on my face. A fusillade followed from behind going over me. If I rose, I knew I was done.

A shotgun boomed, and I looked up to see that flame-haired Sarah Bowman had arrived and taken my side. Juan Largo and Mose Carson stepped into the street grinning and joined the fight.

"Go git 'im, boy!" yelled three-fingered Mose indicating the direction Jacko had run.

"Si, Señor Hombre, he is yours." Juan brought up his pistol and fired up the street.

Limping, I rose and followed Jacko toward the river through tangled mesquite splashing across the *acacia madre*, the mother ditch, the irrigation ditch that fed all others. Thirty paces ahead, Jacko stepped out from behind a cottonwood and fired. I swung left as pain seared through my left arm, and blood spattered my face. A Dragoon Colt fell from my numbed hand. I raised the other and the hammer fell with a click on a spent cylinder or a lost cap. I'd lost count and had no time to check. Dropping the Colt, I reached for the gun in my belt, the one I'd picked up, knowing there wouldn't be time to cock and aim, knowing I was dead.

Seeing Jacko fumbling with a knife, I raised the pistol and aimed. A spent cap had blocked the mechanism of his pistol. He freed it and raised his pistol as I fired and fired again and again until the pistol was empty. The air stank with acrid smoke, and when it cleared Jacko lay dead. He never dropped the pistol or ceased trying to get off a shot. It was time to look for Turk.

I picked up my Dragoons and found that one still had four rounds. I holstered the other and headed back to town gun in my right fist, the left still numb. I didn't look but felt blood dripping from my fingertips and from my wounded thigh. I hurt and tasted blood.

Turk lay near the wagon, his head cradled in Sarah's lap. "Your first shot got him." A wound in his chest bled and bubbled. Pink foam crusted his lips. Juan and Mose stood nearby respectful of a dying man. I tore the cover off the wagon.

Mose glanced into the bed. "Yup, Sharps rifles. Wonder who they're for?"

"They're for Santa Cruz," Turk sputtered and wheezed. "They was 'sposed to go to the 'Patches," he gasped painfully for breath, "but that last shipment got lost." He lapsed into silence, and I thought he was dead.

A gasp alerted me to Alice Ann's presence. By all the saints, she was beautiful, a *fairie* lass. She knelt beside Sarah. "This evil man was selling guns?" she asked.

Sarah pursed her lips. "Been tryin' to tell ya. He's a friend of your fiancé, Robinson."

Alice Ann looked up into my eyes. "Palatine Robinson can't possibly know what his partners were doing."

"He knows," breathed Turk. "He's the boss." A man who enjoyed being cruel, he went on, "And he's got a pretty wife, too."

Alice Ann stood suddenly and looked hatred at Turk. "Did he," pointing at me, "put you up to this?" She stalked away.

Sarah stopped Turk's bleeding and put a piece of wet rawhide over the hole in his chest. "I seen that work once in the Mexico at Buena Vista, but I ain't got much hope for him."

In the night, Turk departed for wherever it was he was going. I thought I smelled brimstone, but it might have been my imagination.

Chapter 32 - There Goes the Neighborhood

When the smoke settled, the wagon train from Sonoita Creek pulled into town from the south along the commercial street that rose along the edge of the bench. It turned west toward the church at Poston's house and parked on the flat west of the Presidio. Below on the river bottoms were scattered homes to the south, the *acacia madre*, mother ditch and fields. To the east, coming close to the town were mesquite *bosques* stretching as far as the Santa Cruz River.

As no one claimed the Sharps rifles in Jacko's wagon, I distributed them to the men of the town and wagon train.

Poston took a rifle but pranced around on tiptoe like a man with an urgent need to visit a bush. "You really shouldn't do that," he said. "Palatine Robinson, he's a powerful man, and he was Jacko's partner."

I glared at the mine owner, and he tried to hold still. "If Palatine wants to complain, he's welcome. He can come right down here and explain how he was selling guns to the Apache and to Mexican outlaws."

The Sharps were a wonder. A man could get off six or ten shots a minute while a man with a rifle could barely manage one or two.

They seemed to appear from nowhere though they must have come through the mesquite. Three Apache stood there calmly looking at me as I handed out rifles. I recognized one, a tall muscular man of about forty dressed in loose white cotton trousers and knee-high moccasins. He was Dragón of the Piñaleno.

In Spanish he said, "Those are my guns. Give them to me."

"Come and take them."

Poston jumped in at my undiplomatic reply. "Perhaps we can work something out. We could give you some of them."

Dragón and I shared a "No!" He wanted all of them, and I as unwilling to give him any.

"Don Palatino has promised us!" Dragón countered growing angry. I hoped Alice Ann was listening, but she probably wasn't.

I looked him hard in the eyes. "Then take it up with him."

"You will all die." Dragón turned and disappeared back into the mesquite.

Poston stammered. "You had no right to speak for all of us. We could have . . ." A shot from the mesquite cut him off, and the siege of Tubac was on.

I tried to rally men to take to the roofs along the main street and those of the Presidio, but most scattered, ducking into buildings. The problem with fighting from the adobes was that there were no windows, and most buildings had only one door. Defenders could barely see out the door in one direction and not that well. They were cut off from each other. I climbed back onto the roof and found two others had done the same. We could control the streets but little else. Trees limited our fields of fire. Before long, daring Apaches were riding down the street and between buildings.

We left them alone until one ran on foot from the mesquite and tried to force the door of the building below me. I couldn't fire without exposing myself by leaning way out over the parapet. A shot from the roof across the street took him and started him on his final journey to wherever Apaches go. If they rushed us, concentrating on one building at a time, we were doomed.

"We need more men up here!" No one answered my plea.

The sun was hot, but as the day wore on, the clouds built up into great mansions in the sky. I stewed in my own sweat, and the skin of my face and hands burned. If we tried to move about, an occasional bullet or arrow reminded us that Apaches were watching our every move. Toward *kindle teening,* the skies broke open, and I drank the rain in an open mouth, delighted to be soaked in the cooling torrent.

The evening was dark when I descended and called people out of the buildings. After we set men in defensive positions, a party worked its way to the well and brought back buckets and canteens of water. We distributed food. Juan Largo and Ole Mose Carson agreed to come up to the roofs. Other men were disinclined to leave their families, but three more joined us. Great Western, Sarah, wanted to come up top, but folks begged her to stay inside with the women. As soon as there were wounded, her help would be needed. Shots rang out, and a man fell wounded and was dragged inside by his family. Sarah followed. The rest of us scattered.

During the night, we got the folks below to hand up chairs and blankets. A blanket stretched from a chair would be protection from the sun in the morning. But first we had to make it through the night. Apaches scurried below in the dark. The streets weren't safe. Fortunately, they don't like to fight in the dark. They fear the monsters that hide in the murk.

Apaches came in force in the false dawn gliding amidst wisps of mist from the river. Shots rang out below. Men fired as Apaches broke in doors. I shot one from behind as he entered a house across the street. There were screams, horrible shrieks, the cries of women and children. I couldn't tell if they were dying or merely frightened.

Unable to stand the cries of terror any longer, I jumped down onto the back of an Apache and finished him with a blow from my heavy Dragoon Colt. Then rising, rushed to the door of a building to find an Apache struggling with one of the men from Sonoita Creek. Pulling the Apache's hair back with one hand, I slit his throat with my Bowie. The man's wife rushed to the settler who was badly wounded. I pulled the Apache outside.

Then as suddenly as it had started, the attack was over.

The light was still too low for effective use of rifle or bow. People emerged for the first time in many hours. We filled buckets and canteens while we could. We checked on each other and found four dead and many wounded. There were two dead Apaches and no wounded. The one I struck down with my Colt had disappeared.

We sent a rider to Tucson for assistance and prayed that he would make it. The Apache were concentrated in the dense mesquite bosques along the river. Away from the river, a rider might stand a chance.

As the sun rose, Alice Ann found me. "I heard what Turk said about the guns and his partner. Can Palatine be as bad as all that?" She threw her arms around me and held me tight. I heard her sob, and the wet on her cheeks soaked my shirt.

As suddenly as she'd come, she let go and ran across the street to her family.

The sun was up now, and Apache snipers started their work. I returned to my roof to bake through the day but happy again for the first time in months. Alice Ann loved me, and I loved her.

Chapter 33 - All Good Things Must Come to an End

The day was hot. Moisture absorbed by the adobe roof became humidity. I parboiled in my own sweat and the steam rising from the roof. The blanket helped keep the sun off, but suspended over the chair, it gave the Apache a target. By midday, it held three arrows. Two more stuck from the roof nearby. A yelp from across the way let me know such a missile had struck one of our defenders. The stream of fluid cursing that followed suggested the man would be all right.

Cooking as I was, my thoughts were equally heated. Alice Ann loved me. She was in love with me again. "Again" because I thought she had loved me for a time when I was courting her. A blessing, thank Saint Peran! But was it? This girl had betrayed me. She didn't trust me. She thought me a beast and ran to a fop. How could I trust her or know she wouldn't do it again? Perhaps it was her age. She was young, a flighty lass. Perhaps she was too young to make a faithful wife. Besides, I was no longer a man of substance. I was a pauper again. Could a young woman follow me down the rugged road to making another fortune, to becoming someone of substance again? How could I ask her to follow me when I didn't know where I was going? Besides, she'd never met and been approved by my parents! Well, there was that, but I wasn't even sure they were still alive. It was a hot day.

Another afternoon storm brought blessed relief. I daydreamed of my elfin beauty and how good it was to have her back. I believed in love at first sight, and I'd loved her since I first saw her. I had to trust her. She would love me and none other. She would be faithful. She would see me for the good man that I am. I would have to be the steady adult for both of us, but I could do that. At least, I was pretty sure I could. I could forgive her. She was just a child.

The sun sank in splendor, all the shades of blood.

In that light, I knew we were star-crossed lovers. The *piskies* or Saint Peran had brought us together. I thanked Saint Peran and as soon as I could, I'd drink a beer in his honor and toast him in beer at my wedding as well.

At dusk, we had a few brief moments on the ground getting water, checking on each other, and setting up a watch. We would shout and toss pebbles from roof to wake each other. Half of us were always awake.

Alice Ann found me again and for a while held me tight. She was wonderful, soft and warm, all I'd ever dreamed of in a wife. Thoughts of any other women fled before the saffron smell of her hair. We didn't talk. It was good to have her back. Too soon our brief moment was over, and she returned to her family and I to my roof.

The night was long, but I got a few hours' sleep.

They came in the false dawn again, silently like the mist. It was eerie. It was as if they were *piskie* creatures. Suddenly, they were among us and breaking down doors.

I fired at a shadow. It twitched and was gone. I fired at another. Juan Largo and Ole Mose were firing from their rooftops, as were the others. The false dawn light was hard to see by, hard to aim by. Every now and then, we'd see a hideous face painted for war that would swirl out of the mist and disappear again. We wasted shots on these ghosts.

There were fights below and screams. It was hard to tell who needed help or who was winning.

The mist swirled aside a moment, and I saw a brave break through the door where Alice Ann's family sheltered. I raised a gun to fire, the hammer clicked on an empty cylinder. I grabbed the other with similar effect. My rifle lay empty. There had been no chance to reload. This was how it felt to be overwhelmed.

I leapt from the roof and, drawing my Bowie, raced to Alice Ann's door. Within I found terrified women and youngsters huddled in a corner. The brave struck Alice Ann's father with his tomahawk, and the elder man fell. I grabbed the hand that held the 'hawk, and the creature twisted about faster than a rattler to confront me with the knife in his other hand. Briefly, we slashed at each, other dueling with our knives. I cut him, and he bled from his side. He returned the compliment and on the backslash cut my hand causing me to drop the weapon.

I caught the wrist that held his knife, and we grappled. Round and round we danced, until I tripped and he fell on top of me. Now he forced his knife to my nose and began slowly to saw across it intent on cutting it off. His thumb passed over my lips.

I opened my mouth and bit down hard and harder still. He made not a cry but released his knife when the digit came off. I kicked with all my might and rolled us over so that I could pin his arms with my knees. Having no weapon but my hands, I choked him into unconsciousness and then took his tomahawk and split his skull.

I rose covered in blood, his and mine, and turned to inspect the women and children. Alice Ann backed away in horror, raising her hands to ward something evil away. I spun and looked behind me. There was nothing there. I turned back toward her. She turned in disgust, revolted, trying to run but stopped by the corner of the adobe. I spit out the thumb.

Outside the shooting had stopped. Either we'd lost, or the Apaches had withdrawn. I grabbed up tomahawk and Bowie and stuck my head out into the street. No one shot it off.

Ole Mose leapt down from his roof. "They've skedaddled again."

I nodded, too tired to speak, and went to bathe my face and hands in the *acacia madre*, irrigation ditch.

Sarah Bowman found me there and bandaged my side and hand. "Need some cobwebs for your nose. I can wrap it but you'll look right ugly." She wrapped it.

I went to check on Alice Ann, and she recoiled from me again in horror. Her father was recovering, his head bandaged and bloody. I went to Alice Ann and knelt beside her only to have her raise hands to face in order to ward me off and squeal. I departed.

Behind me I heard her father's stern voice. "Alice, come here. We need to talk."

In town, we held council. The Apaches had lost only one warrior. The Apache made a great game of playing at being hit and being dead before they came back to life and killed you. They also dragged away their dead and wounded. You never knew how many you'd killed, but it's probably a lot less than you think. We had lost none, this time, but, of course, had more wounded to care for. Wounded were a problem. A dead man was just dead and took himself out of the fight. A wounded man took himself out and usually encumbered at least one other. We couldn't sustain having so many wounded. It was a terrible thought. Tactically we'd be better off if they died. Nonetheless, I couldn't wish them dead. I mumbled a prayer pleading that compassion shouldn't be the cause of our deaths. We were tired and running low on powder and shot.

General Wordsworth stood. "We've lost a few, and we've got wounded. I doubt we can handle another day of this."

Grundy Ake sang to the general's tune. "We's low on powder and ball. Half the doors is busted and won't keep no Injuns out."

The general resumed his theme. "We've got to try to make a break for Tucson."

A man spoke. "We've got livestock to drive. Lots of sheep and cows. We won't be able to go very fast."

Wordsworth replied, "It's a shame, but if we have to, we'll leave them." His statement proved prophetic but not at Tubac as it turned out. The livestock would be lost when Cochise and Mangas Coloradas attacked the wagon train at Cooke's Canyon on the way to the Rio Grande.

Charles Poston had to have his say. "We can't just abandon Tubac!"

I whispered into his ear. "You stay then. We're going." Even in the pale dawn, he looked white.

As we worked loading wagons, gathering flocks and hitching teams, no arrows or shots pursued us.

General Wordsworth called Juan Largo, Mose, and me aside. "What are the Apache planning? Are they waiting until we're strung out on the trail to strike again?"

"Could be," said Mose. "May be tired of us. They don' usual 'tack towns."

"Maybe something scared them off, and they have left," said Juan.

We started out, strung out over half a mile, and hadn't gone a mile up toward the high ground away from the river, when a voice called us back to the rear of the train. "You've got to see this."

Tubac was in flames, at least those parts of it that would burn were.

"Must be Injuns," said Mose rubbing his eyes. "But it don' look like."

Juan Largo spoke up. "It is Mexican banditos from Santa Cruz. They have come to get their rifles, I think."

Voices called us from the head of the train. Turning we saw riders, twenty or so. The relief from Tucson had arrived, and Palatine Robinson was among them.

He sought out Alice Ann. She was calmer now. I could understand her being hysterical when her father was attacked, and I slew the Apache. As I approached, she began running in the other direction. "Alice, are you alright? They didn't harm you, did they?" I called out, but she ignored me.

I ran toward her. But she ran away from me. She got to Palatine Robison before I arrived.

She didn't say a word, but slapped Robinson so hard he fell on his butt. He sat their stunned, rubbing his jaw, which showed a bright red handprint.

I took her arm. She turned and took me in hers, and we stood there holding each other tight.

Somewhere behind me, I heard the Great Western, Sarah Bowman say, "There may be hope for that girl yet." Did I mention that Sarah was a great romantic? Selling love was her business.

I was *piskie* led indeed, but perhaps being blindly led down paths of love would be worth it. Besides, I had no other pressing engagements.

Fin

History behind the story

The background to the story is real, the rivers, mountains, trails and towns are as they were. In July 1861, the Army burned Fort Buchanan and departed for the Rio Grande to repel a Confederate invasion. This caused the evacuation of the Sonoita Valley. Apaches attacked Tubac and after the people left, Mexican raiders looted and burned the town. Captain Richard Ewell served with distinction at Fort Buchanan and elsewhere in New Mexico. He sold his mine, the Patagonia, to Sylvester Mowry who had also served as an officer and who had had to leave Utah after seducing Brigham Young's daughter-in-law. Paddy Graydon served in Ewell's company and after discharge stayed in the area to run the Boundary Hotel. Great Western Sarah Bowman was a camp follower with General Taylor in Mexico and really did all the things related. She went on to run the Casa Blanca. Tevis and Jack Swilling were members of the Arizona Guards or Rangers. Charles Poston was the father of Arizona, a booster and arranger who opened mines in the Santa Ritas. Moses Carson was Kit Carson's older brother and had been a mountain man. For a while, he lived at Tubac. Palatine Robinson was a scoundrel who was jailed for Confederate sympathies. I hope I've captured something of their character and the nature of their adventures.

***The Mystery of Chaco Canyon,* A Review** by Rahm E. Sandoux

The story of Doug Hocking's new historical novel, *The Mystery of Chaco Canyon*, takes place ten years after them events described in his earlier book, *Massacre at Point of Rocks*.

At the bequest of a dying Masonic brother, Dan and his friends Roque, Doña Loca, and Peregrino Rojo, embark on a search for the Los Lunas Decalogue Stone, a boulder with an inscription believed to be an abridged version of the Decalogue (Ten Commandments) in Paleo-Hebrew. The clues lead them all over the Southwest, including the Estancia Valley, Acoma, Zuni, El Morro, the Hopi mesas, the Grand Canyon, Chaco, Chimayo, Chihuahua, and Casas Grandes. They finally locate Rough Hurech's grave in a mountain cave in southwest Arizona and then return to Chaco Canyon.

Along their twisting route, they meet so many minor characters that, to be honest, it was hard for this reader to keep track of them all. Many of these figures are drawn from history, including George Bascom, Padre Antonio Jose Martinez, Kit Carson, and Albert Pike. There are also Danites, Masons Texas Rangers, and Apaches.

Although the plot is motivated by the fictional search, Hocking manages to discuss dozens of historical incidents. These events are described with limited detail, but they might spark a reader's interest to investigate certain incidents more deeply.

The Mystery of Chaco Canyon has all the elements that endeared Hocking's previous book to Southern Trails Chapter readers: short chapters broken into even shorter scenes that make it easy to say to yourself, "I'll just read one more chapter," and before you know it, you are swept up in another bit of exciting action.

Hocking clearly loves history, and in *The Mystery of Chaco Canyon*, he demonstrates a knowledge of and appreciation for the various cultures inhabiting the Southwest.

Rahm E. Sandoux

A page from
Massacre at Point of Rocks

Going West on the Santa Fe Trail

The affair ended in blood and icy death for Indian and white alike. How strange that chance meetings and hasty words of no more weight than seeds of *chamisa* dusting the fall breeze should bring so many to calamity. Bad acts and actors abounded. Small things, done by people meaning well enough, led to disaster for everyone, but through it all, a boy grew and moved toward manhood.

He was tall for his age and broad shouldered, nearly a man and working his first real job. Insulated by school and native intelligence, he used his wits to escape the lessons apprenticed boys and laborers learned early working with men. Possessing the body of an adult he had not yet fully matured as many younger than he had already done. Still expecting men to be the bold, perfect heroes in his books, he was disappointed by the imperfections of real men. The West was the land of his heroes. He would find a man to look up to on the Frontier. He was called Danny

Trelawney, or more often by the men of the slow moving caravan, *Danito*. They trudged, their wagons four abreast, through dust and sweat following the long, dry road to Santa Fe, which stood in imagination and dreams a gleaming citadel of wealth and exotic sight, sounds, and smells. Santa Fe was where men made their fortunes. Danito thought of it as the home of Kit Carson and a place where folks met wild Indians.

He walked behind an ox team, whip in hand and cracking it now and then above a beast's back as warning to keep moving. He was lucky to have this job occasioned by a man's demise. The sickness was a mystery to those in the caravan. Fortunately, it took no one else, but death on the trail was all too common. The men who ran the *ramuda*, the horse and mule herd, were all New Mexicans, so the boy wouldn't fit there. The cooks were Cajuns and Quebec French speaking a language few but they could understand. The boy replaced the one who had died walking beside an ox team.

What kind folks have said about
Massacre at Point of Rocks

Historian Will Gorenfeld said: Very readable and informative. Your knowledge and description of Aubrey's train, the men, the countryside is, thus far, superb as is Grier's failed attempt to rescue Mrs. White.

Author Gerald Summers said: Doug Hocking has done himself proud. His writing flows smoothly, his historical references are spot on, and his action exciting. I recently read Kit Carson's autobiography and found it to be one of the most interesting historical presentations I've ever read. And that is saying something, for I have studied western history for many years. Doug has captured much of this famous man and his exploits and deserves much credit for bringing him and his other wonderful characters to life. I thoroughly enjoyed this book.

Jicarilla Apache teacher from Dulce, NM, on the Jicarilla Reservation said: Written by a resident of the community - interesting story line. Reading parts to my Middle and High School classes in hopes to spark their reading interests.

Shar Porier of the Sierra Vista Herald said: It [reveals] an historical view of the life and times in New Mexico in the 1840s and '50s in a novel story, written just as one produced by western authors of the past. It is hard to set the book aside.

Greg Coar: Just finished your book. Saved it for the trip home. Loved it. Hope there is more to come. Great to meet you and your wife in Tombstone. Keep the history coming.

Dac Crassley of the Old West Daily Reader: As you know, I have a considerable interest in Western History and enough knowledge to make me dangerous. And I read a lot because of my research for Old West Daily Reader. This book was comfortable, like worn in buckskins or one's favorite Levis. Everything felt right. The story unfolded in a coherent and, for me, personal fashion. I truly appreciated and enjoyed your obvious care in building the historical background of the tale. Characters were fleshed out, real, believable. I could picture the landscapes. The trail dust…Ok, I really liked the book! Great accomplishment and a fine telling!

Rahm E. Sandoux, *Desert Tracks* (OCTA) reviewer: Doug Hocking's *Massacre at Point of Rocks* is a fascinating story of historic events along the Santa Fe Trail in 1849. Setting the White massacre and captivity in context, Hocking reveals to readers the ethnic side of of the frontier, showing how Indians, Mexicans, and blacks were just as much a part of that historical tapestry as the white men were. He brings characters like Kit Carson, Grier, Comancheros, and the Jicarilla Apaches to life, revealing how tough life was on the frontier for all of its inhabitants. *Massacre at Point of Rocks* will definitely be of interest to readers who want to learn more about the history of New Mexico and the Santa Fe Trail.

About the Author

Doug Hocking grew up on the Jicarilla Apache Reservation in the Rio Arriba (Northern New Mexico). He attended reservation schools, an Ivy League prep school, and graduated from high school in Santa Cruz, New Mexico, in the Penitente heartland among *paisonos* and *Indios*. Doug enlisted in Army Intelligence out of high school and worked in Taiwan, Thailand and at the Pentagon. Returning home he studied Social Anthropology (Ethnography) and then returned to the Army as an Armored Cavalry officer (scout) completing his career by instructing Military Intelligence lieutenants in intelligence analysis and the art of war.

He has earned a master's degree with honors in American History and completed field school in Historical Archaeology. Since retiring he has worked with allied officers and taught at Cochise College. He is now an independent scholar residing in southern Arizona near Tombstone with his wife, dogs, a feral cat and a friendly coyote. In 2016, Arizona Governor Doug Ducey appointed him to the board of the Arizona Historical Society. He is Vice President for Arizona of the Southern Trails Chapter of the Oregon-California Trails Association, a Road Scholar for Arizona Humanities and Sheriff of the Cochise County Corral of the Westerners.

Doug has published in *Wild West*, *True West*, *Buckskin Bulletin* and *Roundup Magazine.* He has three novels in print: ***Massacre at Point of Rocks*** about Kit Carson and the White wagon train massacre, ***The Mystery of Chaco Canyon*** concerning mystery, archaeology and lost treasure, and ***Devil on the Loose***, a story of love and adventure in 1860 Arizona. The is also an anthology of short material,

The Wildest West. He is working on a biography of *Tom Jeffords, Cochise's Friend.*

All books are available at www.doughocking.com , on Amazon.com and through Ingram.